Hayner Public Library District-Alton

W9-BKG-939

RECEIVED
APR 2 1 2005
BY:_____ MAIN

HAYNER PUBLIC LIBRARY DISTRICT
ALTON, ILLINOIS

OVERDUES .10 PER DAY MAXIMUM FINE
COST OF BOOKS. LOST OR DAMAGED
BOOKS ADDITIONAL $5.00 SERVICE CHARGE.

# Glimmering Girls

**Library of American Fiction**

The University of Wisconsin Press Fiction Series

# Glimmering Girls

## A Novel of the Fifties

## Merrill Joan Gerber

THE UNIVERSITY OF WISCONSIN PRESS

HAYNER PUBLIC LIBRARY DISTRICT
ALTON, ILLINOIS

The University of Wisconsin Press
1930 Monroe Street
Madison, Wisconsin 53711

www.wisc.edu/wisconsinpress/

3 Henrietta Street
London WC2E 8LU, England

Copyright © 2005
The Board of Regents of the University of Wisconsin System
All rights reserved

1     3     5     4     2

Printed in the United States of America

Library of Congress Cataloging-in-Publication Data
Gerber, Merrill Joan.
Glimmering girls: a novel of the fifties / Merrill Joan Gerber.
    p.     cm.—(Library of American fiction)
    ISBN 0-299-21060-X (cloth: alk. paper)
    1. Nineteen fifties—Fiction.   I. Title.   II. Series.
        PS3557.E664G58        2005
        813′.54—dc22        2004023302

Terrace Books, a division of the University of Wisconsin Press,
takes its name from the Memorial Union Terrace, located
at the University of Wisconsin–Madison. Since its inception in 1907,
the Wisconsin Union has provided a venue for students, faculty, staff,
and alumni to debate art, music, politics, and the issues of the day.
It is a place where theater, music, drama, dance, outdoor activities,
and major speakers are made available to the campus and the community
To learn more about the Union, visit www.union.wisc.edu.

F
GER

AEW-9682

**For my friends, Girls of the fifties**

Myra Marcus

Barbara Katz

Eleanor Katz

Helen Lachman

Martha Schrage

# Contents

1    Hall Meeting, University of Florida, 1959     3
2    Teachers of Life     13
3    The Land of Love     20
4    Grease Monkeys     27
5    Party Kitchen     38
6    Shellfish     46
7    Panty Raid     52
8    Fluff     61
9    Sermon     67
10   Letter Home (1)     74
11   Playing House     80
12   By Firelight     91
13   *Tosca*     96
14   Every Pot Has a Cover     105
15   Music of the Spheres     113
16   Letter Home (2)     125
17   The Bench     133
18   *La Bohème*     142

| 19 | Gynecology | 149 |
| 20 | Collusion | 158 |
| 21 | Peachtree Lake | 166 |
| 22 | Terror | 177 |
| 23 | The Other World | 186 |
| 24 | The Hazel Wood | 193 |
| 25 | Cross Creek | 199 |
| 26 | Purge | 205 |
| 27 | Phi Beta Kappa | 215 |
| 28 | "You Women Have a Habit . . ." | 219 |
| 29 | New York, New York | 224 |
| 30 | Life! | 232 |
| 31 | There's No Stopping Me Now | 239 |
| 32 | Land of Hope and Glory | 244 |

# Glimmering Girls

# I

# Hall Meeting, University of Florida, 1959

Francie's roommate, Mary Ella Root, sits like a small, dense rhinoceros on her bed, reading Bride's magazine. Behind her, through the window of their third-floor dorm room, moonlight showers down upon the silvery needles of an arrow-shaped pine tree. Much further away, invisible in the distant dark, is the long country road leading north from Florida, through Georgia, the Carolinas, and beyond, to the great crowded city of Francie's birth, New York.

Fate, the fickle hand of fortune, and her family's necessities have conspired to transplant Francie to a land where the trees grow beards, where handsome, crew-cut boys say "Ma'am" to all females, and where—on the cafeteria line at the student union—she gets grits shoveled onto her plate as a matter of course before she can decline them.

"Honey, throw me that bag of Tootsie Pops from my desk, would you, angel?"

Where Mary Ella's ears would normally appear are two fat foam-rubber rollers, and strapped under her chin is her Face Lifter, an underwear-pink device of elastic guaranteed to tighten the little hammock of flesh that Mary Ella swears is hereditary, the feature with which all her female ancestors have been cursed. ("But even so," she tells Francie frequently, "most of them caught men, and, in a few cases, two apiece!") She laughs as she always does when referring to her holy quest: finding a husband before graduation. After graduation, the odds fall to zero: she'll be a second-grade teacher with no one to meet but other women teachers. "It's a rule of nature," Mary Ella has explained, "that all elementary school principals are married men."

Francie is supposed to become a teacher, too. A teacher or a nurse—that's about all there is for girls. Unless she gets married, and then a girl doesn't have to be anything. Her parents assume she intends to be a teacher. Even now, in her senior year, Francie hasn't had the heart to tell them otherwise.

But Francie does marvel at her roommate: how can Mary Ella be so cheerful, so optimistic, despite her dim prospects, despite her months of dateless Saturday nights? She talks nonstop, to herself, to no one, as she flips the magazine pages, comparing bridal fashions, interrupting Francie incessantly regardless of her protestations that she is trying to write a paper on *Sons and Lovers* for Dr. Reynold's Classics of Fiction class.

"I wonder if I should choose big puffed sleeves, or the long skinny kind of satin with the lacy point down over the wrist. An embroidered pearl bodice is so feminine, but maybe lace is more graceful. Which would you choose, Francie?"

"If I were you, I'd probably wait to decide till I found myself a bridegroom. Styles may have changed by then."

"Oh, I doubt it," Mary Ella says. "Wedding gowns are classic. They last for generations. Maybe for all eternity."

"Like love," Francie intones. She can't help herself— she rolls her eyes heavenward. She is glad her back is toward her roommate. "Like true love."

"Oh, yes," Mary Ella sighs. "And we must never despair. There's a cover for every pot, you know."

"What if your juices boil away before you find the right one?"

"Honey—I don't know what you mean."

"Never mind. It's only metaphor, Mary Ella. I think in metaphors when I'm trying to write a paper."

✳

She cannot in good conscience belittle Mary Ella's devotion to Bride's magazine. In notes taken in her biology class last week, she recorded the pronouncement of her professor, a published expert on the subject, that an overpowering drive to mate exists in the human condition and is known as "the biological imperative." As if to submit proof for this theorem, this very afternoon, in the very same biology class, while peering into her microscope, Francie experienced this truth firsthand. On her slide, an amoeba, while dividing itself, presented to Francie's eyes the sudden appearance of what seemed to be a male sexual organ, engorged, in conjunction with a similar female receptacle. The male organ seemed to be injecting, by rhythmic pulsations, its contents into the welcoming orifice of its counterpart.

Suddenly faint, overwhelmed by an imperative she would not have previously been able to name, Francie excused herself from the classroom and, in a cubicle in the restroom—barely leaning against the metal paper dispenser—had a brief, involuntary orgasm. Her body rushed through the various ascending levels without her consent; she had not even to form a single helpful thought. The tornado that overcame her blew away as fast as it had appeared. Delivered once again to a rational state, she washed her face, took a number of deep breaths, and returned immediately to class, where she took her place before her microscope. She studied the proceedings on the slide and continued to take notes, using her ruler to underline primary headings. She was trembling.

Something had taken her by the hand, some

inherent teacher of life, to prove to her how clear it was that reproduction ruled the world.

✗

Just as Francie is getting her thoughts to a point where she might type a complete opening sentence on the page, the emergency bells go off. Within two minutes a hall monitor is pounding the door.

"Meeting in Broward Lobby! Everyone downstairs right now! Be at the hall meeting or be grounded!"

"Hell's bells," Mary Ella moans. Once she has grounded her self in bed, covered with beauty creams, her toenails separated by cotton balls in preparation for being painted with a little brush, her teddy bears and her other childhood sacraments lined up in their rows, moving herself out of there is like moving a continent.

"Go for me, Francie, you can tell me what they want."

"They'll know you're not there, Mary Ella. The floor monitor takes roll! They'll ground you. Then you won't be able to go out on the weekend."

"That's what I want!" she says, in her good-natured way. "If I'm grounded, then no one knows I don't have a date."

"Maybe you'll get a date and then you'll be sorry you can't go out."

"You think there'll be a miracle, Francie? You're Jewish. I didn't think the Jewish people believe in miracles."

"Well, not specific miracles. I mean, Jews don't pray to get a date or to get an idea for a term paper. Jewish miracles are mostly about seas parting and bushes burning, events useful for a whole religious group. But, listen, I have to go down now."

Francie throws her quilted bathrobe over her baby doll pajamas and tells Mary Ella to guard the fort. She joins the throng headed for the lobby, taking a few sheets of notebook paper, her copy of *Sons and Lovers,* and some chocolate kisses, which she drops in the pocket of her robe.

✻

She can never get over the herd of females who live here, the sound of their clattering feet stampeding down the slanted ramps, the bubbly hysteria of their high-pitched cries. They seem to share an intensity of pur-pose, a total devotion to their quest to achieve beauty and, therefore, by simple logic, to conquer men. All of them by this time of night have tortured their hair into some type of contraption: if they have not skewered it in hair pins, they have spiraled it in rollers, or corseted it in rubber bands, or bound it in circlets, or tacked it with bobby pins, or pressed it tight under sailor hats, or rounded it into pageboys over sausages of toilet paper stuffed into skins of old nylon stockings. This effort of molding and shaping is to affect a natural result for the next day's hunting.

Francie almost imagines she hears in the lobby the

sound of hounds gathering for the hunt, waiting to be freed from confinement so that they may set upon their quarry. Reaching the lobby where the hall meeting will be held, she takes her position among them.

✗

The emergency concerns the discovery that toilet paper is being used for the blotting of lipstick. The house-mother, Mrs. Taylor, has discovered, all around the bathrooms, little angel wings of toilet paper fluttering in the air currents with the imprint of kissing lips on them.

"The state budget does not allow such abundant funding for the blotting of lipstick; the state pays only for the purpose for which toilet paper is designed. Do we girls understand? Will we continue to abuse the privilege of undoled-out toilet paper? Or would we prefer to check out and sign for a packet of little paper squares each week?"

No, we would not, is the obvious answer. Mrs. Taylor, a middle-aged woman with her gray hair in pin-curls, seems very upset, indeed; she has been betrayed by her charges' profligate use of paper, she has a feeling of deep personal shame that the young women for whom she is responsible are not well behaved.

"It's as if I haven't taught you manners, girls!" Her face is strained and sad. She has been there and back, to where the girls long to go. She holds herself before the throng as a model for each one of them, a walking outline of what may befall every woman here: love, marriage, children—then the ugly swipe of the scythe, and a woman is undone. Widowed and bereft, not only does she have to take a job in a dormitory, guarding an army of recalcitrant virgins, but she must police the wasting and misuse of toilet paper, as well.

"Do you girls realize that this investigation into our supplies is a blot on my name?" she cries, raising her eyes heavenward, where they light upon something that causes her to gasp. Francie and the other young women follow her gaze. On a ceiling light fixture shaped to look like a candelabra hangs a limp, white, rubbery tube.

Someone names it in a whisper. The girls begin to scream. Francie has never seen one of these, but she knows what it must be. Pandemonium is breaking out. The girls are screeching and rushing about the room, seeking their friends and falling against them and screeching again. One girl appears to faint upon a couch. Mrs. Taylor throws her pen at the object, which clings tenaciously to a bulb shaped like a candle flame. She cannot dislodge it.

Francie is transfixed by the spectacle. Is she really of the same species as these girls? Is she really programmed by nature to jump and scream and shriek and wiggle her behind?

At this moment, her eyes fall upon two girls who are sitting motionless on a couch, taking in the panorama with wide, slightly stern eyes. She and they exchange glances. Their expressions are bemused, ironic. Pure intelligence shines out of their faces. They seem to invite her into their camp. In any case, she finds herself walking toward them, as to an island of sanity.

"Can you believe this?" one of them says to Francie.

"College life," says the other.

"Girls will be girls," says the first. Both of them are fair, delicate as pastel angels, glowing. They look lighted from within.

Does Francie know them? They seem more than familiar, as if they speak the language of her interior spaces.

Around them in the lobby, the riot is still going on. Mrs. Taylor has run to her apartment, apparently to call maintenance for help, to have someone (a man, it can't be helped) bring a ladder and remove the hideous object. A circle of girls is trying to revive the girl on the couch; they fan her, they bring her a paper cup of water.

Francie, for comfort, reaches into the pocket of her robe, feeling for the chocolate kisses rubbing against one another in their silvery tear-shaped wrappers. She holds out her palm, offering them to her new friends. Each girl accepts and unwraps one.

"Say, would you like to come up to our room for a while? Liz was going to play some guitar before this emergency broke out."

"Well, I don't know . . . ," Francie says. "I have a paper to write." She indicates her copy of *Sons and Lovers*.

"Don't we all?" says the one who must be Liz. She wears her gold hair in a short, shimmering cap.

"Come just for a while," says the other girl, whose hair is incredibly long, like the hair of princesses in fairy tale books. Not only does it cascade, but it tumbles, it falls in ringlets and waves and ribbons of light.

"We can discuss *Anna Karenina*," says Liz, revealing to Francie the reason she senses she already knows them—both of them sit across the room in her Russian literature class.

"I'm Amanda," says the girl with golden tresses.

"And I'm Francie."

"Good name," both girls remark at the same time.

"We like good solid names," Amanda adds. "Not Lizzy. Not Mandy."

"Not Franny," says Francie, though she doubts this reasoning will hold.

"Exactly," says Liz, sweeping her bathrobe regally over the lobby rug. "You understand what's important. So come on up with us. This urgent hall meeting seems to have adjourned. Let's arise and retreat to the privacy of our palace."

Francie follows the girls up the rubber ramp. A red carpet seems to unroll before them, just as it seems to Francie that Liz and Amanda are wearing golden crowns on their golden heads. Up they go to their fourth-floor room, their palace, at whose threshold Francie hesitates, then enters.

# 2

# Teachers of Life

Their room is just like Francie's and Mary Ella Root's. Two beds, two desks, two chairs; two trunks, two radios, two lamps. But three girls. Francie, feeling like a third wheel, looks for a place to sit. Liz is perched on the edge of her bed with her guitar already balanced on her knees. Amanda has flung herself, face up, on her bed and crossed her hands over her breasts, as if she were the decoration on her own tomb.

Liz strokes the hiplike curves of the guitar, lightly brushes her fingertips over the strings. "Francie," she says, "we need to ask you one thing. We hope you don't mind, but we have to find out if you're an education major. We seem to have a problem with anyone who has chosen the Required Path for All Decent Young

Women. The truth is, Amanda and I just can't be friends with education majors."

"I'm a lapsed education major," Francie confesses. "I had to give up on it. In my freshman year I took music education, and I learned how to play 'Three Blind Mice' on the autoharp. In my second year, I took art education, and I learned how to finger-paint and glue straws and seashells to a shoe box. Then, last year, when I was a junior, I took the required education observation course, where you have to visit an hour a day at the elementary school. You pick one child to observe, and you write down everything he does. My little boy knew I was watching him. Every child in that class knew there was one adult in the back row writing down everything he did! Day after day, all my boy did was sit there. Then, one day, he brought a switchblade to class and flashed it at me with a really evil grin. I think he wanted to be sure I'd have something interesting to write in my notebook."

"Smart little kid," Liz says. "But we're glad you aren't going to go over the cliff with the other lemmings. Amanda and I got out, too. We couldn't bear all that nonsense. Don't ask us what we'll do after graduation; we haven't the faintest idea."

"We better figure out something by the end of the year," Francie says. "Or we'll all end up being typists."

"Heaven forbid," Amanda says.

"Actually, I like to type," Francie says. "Writers

type, too. James Joyce typed his books. Hemingway typed his."

"But not Emily Dickinson. Not Tolstoy."

"Not Thomas Wolfe, either, I think. He wrote leaning on his refrigerator."

"Well, pull up a chair, Francie," Liz says. She leans over and slides her desk chair out. Then, without further preliminaries, she begins to play her guitar. She bends her head over the strings and in a high, pure voice, begins to sing:

*I went out to the hazel wood,*
*Because a fire was in my head,*
*And cut and peeled a hazel wand,*
*And hooked a berry to a thread;*
*And when white moths were on the wing,*
*And moth-like stars were flickering out,*
*I dropped the berry in a stream*
*And caught a little silver trout.*

She pauses to look up at Francie; "That's 'The Song of Wandering Aengus,' W. B. Yeats." Her hands return to pluck the strings, her long neck tilts gracefully over the shining wood.

*When I had laid it on the floor*
*I went to blow the fire aflame,*
*But something rustled on the floor,*
*And someone called me by my name:*
*It had become a glimmering girl*
*With apple blossom in her hair*
*Who called me by my name and ran*
*And faded through the brightening air.*

"I'll tell you one thing," says Amanda. "If that fellow out in the hazel wood caught me on his line and asked me to surrender my virginity to him, I would, in one second flat. I used to think I would save myself till I was twenty-seven, and after that I'd be so old it wouldn't matter. But now I think if I met a man who was a genius, who really saw the apple blossom in my hair, I would give it all away, just like that." Amanda closes her eyes and adds, "Of course, only if I could get some safe birth control."

Francie takes the opportunity of this intermission to glance around the room, hunting for other clues about these girls' lives—looking for framed photographs of boyfriends, for crucifixes or childhood dolls or high-heeled shoes, for perfume and makeup, for pennants and talismans. But she finds nothing significant, and her eyes are drawn back to Liz as she begins to sing again:

*Though I am old with wandering*
*Through hollow lands and hilly lands,*
*I will find out where she has gone,*
*And kiss her lips and take her hands;*
*And walk among long dappled grass,*
*And pluck till time and times are done*
*The silver apples of the moon,*
*The golden apples of the sun.*

Liz sighs and sets the guitar down gently at the side of her bed.

"Oh, where is Wandering Aengus on this campus?" whispers Amanda. "I'd sell my soul for him . . . even if he is old with wandering."

"Age is meaningless," Liz says, " . . . under the eye of eternity."

Francie's head is turning from one to the other as if she is watching a ping pong game. This is not the kind of talk she hears in other rooms up and down the corridors of Broward Hall. Nothing she and her roommate say to each other resembles this kind of deep communion. How come she and Mary Ella Root don't discuss profound and philosophical matters?

"We have very high ideals," Amanda remarks to Francie as if she has read her mind. She turns on her side so that a curtain of her blonde hair hangs over the edge of the bed. "But we aren't ordinary romantics, Francie. We want transcendent love. We don't respond to the kind of men the other girls go nuts over. For example, we think Elvis Presley is repulsive. All that phlegm in his throat. However, we do adore T. S. Eliot, we kiss the feet of Proust."

"What about Thomas Wolfe?" Francie ventures. "I like him. He's not bad, is he?"

"Infantile," says Liz. "A self-absorbed enormous, whining baby."

"How about D. H. Lawrence? Is he self-absorbed? He seems very smart."

"He's a genius about sex. Did you read his story 'The Fox'? How he makes the tree fall on that pesty girl? And how he uses the fox's tail as a phallic symbol? You do know what that is, don't you, Francie? Phallic symbols are all the rage in English classes this year," Liz tells her.

"Not in Dr. Reynold's Classics of Fiction class."

"Would you like to read some real D. H. Lawrence?" Amanda whispers. "What do you think, Liz?"

They glance conspiratorially at one another.

"I wouldn't rush her," Liz says to Amanda. Then she turns to Francie. "The fact is, Francie, we're invited to a party this weekend. Our friend Reginald, he's the editor of *The Alligator Review,* he somehow got hold of a copy of *Lady Chatterley's Lover* smuggled here from Paris. You know the book's been banned in this country. Well, he's promised to show it around at his party. Things could get out of hand, Francie, and we don't know if you're ready for this."

"I could get ready," Francie says at once, and as soon as the words are spoken she recognizes how tired she is of dormitory existence, how weary of living among girls whose ultimate goal is to be asked for a date by some shallow, crew-cut college boy. She has had, she must acknowledge, like Mary Ella Root, an essentially dateless college life. In three years, she has been to no homecoming dances, fraternity parties, jitterbug contests, football bashes. She has not gotten drunk at Linden Lake, or run across the stadium with a bucket on her head, or dumped red paint on the SAE mascot, the lion that decorates the frat house. Twice she has been to an art movie with a boy in some class of hers who found himself with an extra ticket to the show, and she did once get asked to a concert by a bassoon player. But a date, the archetypal, college-girl date with a college boy, this full-fledged, highly touted, much desired, bigger-than-life entity has evaded her grasp. Not that she particularly longs for the experience. Surely there must be a goal greater than getting a date and ultimately having a gossamer tulle wedding veil hanging over her face. Surely a greater future can be hoped for than is routinely imagined in a dormitory girl's dream. But how is it Liz and Amanda managed to dip their toes into another universe?

If they will have her, Francie decides, she will be led by them. She will gladly choose them to enlighten her, to be her teachers of life.

"Yes," she says, as if a long debate is over. "I'm ready for everything."

# 3

# The Land of Love

At the party to which Francie has allowed herself to be taken, the furniture consists mainly of mattresses on the floor, derelict doors laid over orange crates that serve as tables, large empty wine bottles made into lamps, and small empty wine bottles pretending to be candleholders. Full wine bottles, glowing red with drink, are passed around in ritual seriousness, moving from hand to hand as each guest pours himself a paper cupful.

Francie finds it awkward to sit on the edge of a mattress (whose stuffing is coming out from rips in the striped, stained cloth), awkward to keep her knees in a decent position. If she lets them fall to the side, her spine feels wrenched; if she brings them up straight, she has to hold her dress close to her body under her thighs.

The men, of course, with their protective trousers, can sit any which way, legs spread, knees splayed, their hands free for other purposes. Even holding herself motionless, Francie feels like a balancing act, up on a high wire, with the crowd below looking up her dress.

Their host, Reginald, is wearing a beret; a little goatee sprouts from his chin. He's short and dense; his broad, hairy chest is visible through his open shirt. In his pudgy hands he holds several issues of *The Alligator Review,* the literary journal he edits. His wife, Lulu, is hugely pregnant in overalls; she waves a cigarette holder in the air when she speaks. Francie conjures up a picture of this married couple in the nether reaches of their ratty apartment, together in a double bed where they make love, probably naked. Can such a tattered-looking, un-attractive, scraggly looking duo engage in the infamous act of love and by so doing actually experience a spiritual joining of their souls? Could these two actually transcend their gritty, tacky surroundings and rise up to the starry heights of sublime poetry?

As Francie glances around the room, she notes that the bohemians are passing cubes of American cheese around in a frying pan with a black wooden handle. When the pan gets to her, she gingerly lifts a sticky lump and tries to chew it. It adheres to her palate, and she imagines she may actually suffocate before she can dislodge it. She only hopes no one is watching the contortions her mouth is making.

Other than Amanda and Liz, she doesn't know a

soul here, and she's ended up far across the room from her friends. Liz is deep in conversation with a man who has stretched out on one of the mattresses. He squints into the glare coming down from the bare light bulb above him, his face pained, until Liz moves over him to shade his eyes with the shadow of her head. The motion is so intimate and private that Francie knows at once this is Liz's boyfriend. He looks totally familiar to Francie, like one of her Jewish cousins—handsome, with round eyeglasses and dark curly hair. She knows already what he likes to eat and how his mother raised him. He is clearly transfixed by Liz's moving lips. What can she be saying to him?

Francie has the sense she's in a submarine and it's slowly submerging, going down into deep, dark waters.

✷

When a man sits down on the mattress beside her, he offers her a leather-bound book and points to a page of it. "Listen to this," he says and begins to read, almost directly into her ear, so that she feels his hot breath fanning her hair:

*"Without knowing, he came quickly towards her and crouched beside her again, taking the chick from her hands, because she was afraid of the hen, and putting it back in the coop. At the back of his loins the fire suddenly darted stronger."*

"Why are you reading this to me?" Francie asks.

"Listen to it," insists the man. "It's famous." He

begins to read again, and, at the same time, almost in a hypnotic trance, he very slowly moves his hand over to rest on Francie's kneecap.

*"His heart melted suddenly, like a drop of fire, and he put out his hand and laid his fingers on her knee."*

She, feeling the man's fingers on her knee, says, "Is this . . . ? Can this be *Lady Chatterley's Lover*!"

He nods. His eyes seem to brim in the immensity of the moment. "It gets better," he says. "Listen." In a deep, seductive voice, he reads on, squeezing Francie's knee for emphasis:

*"She lay quite still, in a sort of sleep, in a sort of dream. Then she quivered as she felt his hand groping softly, yet with queer thwarted clumsiness among her clothing. Yet the hand knew, too, how to unclothe her where it wanted. He drew down the thin silk sheath, slowly, carefully, right down over her feet. Then with a quiver of exquisite pleasure he touched the warm soft body, and touched her navel for a moment in a kiss. And he had to come into her at once, to enter the peace on earth of her soft, quiescent body. It was the moment of pure peace for him, the entry into the body of a woman."*

"Pure peace," the man whispers into Francie's ear. They are both breathing hard. Francie tries to make out the face of the man, but her head is spinning from too much wine. His hand is still on her leg, moving up her thigh. His fingers suddenly dart upward and brush a place where no one has ever touched her. She draws her breath in sharply. Limp and without volition, she remembers the amoeba shape under the microscope. She's helpless. She's ready to go behind one of those curtained doorways with him, to whatever biological imperative awaits her.

The man stands and offers her his hand. She lets him pull her to an erect position. She begins to follow him wherever he will lead her. At that instant, the room is doused with a rainbow of floodlights.

"Reginald," announces Reginald's pregnant wife in overalls, "is going to read some of his new poems. Let's give this artist *nonpareil* a big hand!"

The poet, his eyes bloodshot, takes his wife's pungent cigarette, waves it in the air in its long holder, and begins to read. Francie, stopped in her tracks, tries to make sense of the words, but all she hears is a babble of impenetrable, multisyllabic nonsense.

The Mattress Man, who has been gripping her hand, suddenly lets go and begins migrating across the room to where a new hill of cheese cubes has materialized and is being passed around on a cracked plate.

"Having a good time?" someone whispers in Francie's ear, and she turns to see Liz beside her, feels Liz's hand touch her back gently. Her touch feels like a benediction, a blessing. Francie almost takes her friend's fingers and kisses them. She makes an attempt to reel in the fraying thread of her self-control. My God! What if she had succumbed so easily, capitulated without a second thought, given away her virginity, her very soul, to the faceless Mattress Man?

"Come with me," Liz says, taking her hand. "I want you to meet . . . some friends."

Parting some hanging beads with a sharp jangle, Liz thrusts Francie through the portal. There, in a tiny room, she sees two beautiful young men who are paper cutouts of each other. Their faces and forms are identical. She looks around for the trick mirror, the magician, the sorcerer who is trifling with her, but these beings seem real, corporeal. Their legs are as long as stilts, their hips slender, their shoulders wide and powerful-looking. Their temples, shorn of hair in the crew-cut style of the day, reveal delicate veins under tender skin, making the skulls beneath seem extremely vulnerable.

"Meet my special twins." Liz whispers in her ear.

"Yours?"

"Yes. They are unique in all the world."

Francie recognizes those words from *Le Petit Prince;* with these very words, the Little Prince describes the flower he adores. Francie immediately adores the beautiful twins. She tries to steady herself against the wall. Is she quite drunk?

The twins smile at her with their identical faces. They look over her head at each other in a manner so intimate that she is filled with awe. She guesses, with sudden, overwhelming grief, that they must never be lonely, as she always is.

"Bobby and Jerry, meet Francie," Liz says.

They dip their beautiful heads toward Francie, each leaning to place an arm against the wall behind her head. Their faces seem kind, monkey-like, full of animal curiosity.

"Francie," Liz says, as if she is giving away the world, "meet my twins."

# 4

# Grease Monkeys

Francie, studying for a test in Liz and Amanda's room on a weekday afternoon, hears the two girls sing a refrain over and over, without guitar accompaniment, more potent than any stanza of Yeats:

*Bobby and Jerry*
*Bobby and Jerry*
*Bobby and Jerry*

From time to time they add an additional lyric:

*Bill, Bobby, and Jerry*
*Bill, Bobby, and Jerry*
*Bill, Bobby, and Jerry*

They are like bees in a jar, buzzing these names, over and over, while Francie calmly attempts to study, waiting for her guides to announce the next move they will make. She is content in her new privilege of being allowed to be here, not unwelcome but quite the opposite. Liz and Amanda seem pleased to have her under their tutelage, attentive and acquiescent.

"Bobby and Jerry are taking the Alvis out on the Waldo Road to see how fast it can go."

"Bobby and Jerry are going into Jacksonville with Bill to see if they can get parts for the Alvis."

"Let's go over to the Piggly Wiggly and see if we can buy some Alvis Jelly to surprise Bobby and Jerry with."

Francie wonders: what is this Alvis, and is it anything like Elvis? Does it have too much phlegm in its throat? And what about Alvis jelly? (Does it have something to do with contraceptive jelly, a word much whispered around the dormitory as a modern miracle, the one thing that can save a girl from pregnancy, but only with that other mysterious object—a diaphragm—that can be obtained only at a doctor's office and only prior to one's wedding.)

And what about these men, the Bill, Bobby, and Jerry of the recurring refrain: to whom do they belong, if anyone here, and is one of them for Francie? (She knows part of the answer to that question—Bill, the one who could be Francie's Jewish cousin, is clearly bound to Liz.)

Yet Francie is happy to bide her time; all things will be revealed, and in the meantime she is totally available. If Liz and Amanda go somewhere, Francie goes with them. If they express a fierce opinion about some outrage they share, Francie is glad to second it. If accepting their system of belief will take her into new worlds, she is packed and ready to go. There is nothing to leave behind but Mary Ella Root in her bed with her beauty devices.

"So let's go right now to the Piggly Wiggly," Liz says, and it is done. The three of them slam shut their books and depart the room.

✷

They walk quickly across the campus, Liz's leather-heeled loafers tapping smartly on the cement path. Both Liz and Amanda are dressed in pleated wool skirts and cashmere sweater sets. Little white Peter Pan collars peek out of the round necklines of their pink sweaters.

Francie wears a quilted circle skirt that seems excessive to her; pounds of blanket-like material swirl around her legs and catch between her thighs. All three girls wear thick white socks with ribbed tops, folded over, ankle-high. Francie regrets the weight of her basket bag, woven of thin strips of wood—an unwieldy contraption with its stiff wooden handle, its two lids that fold back on hinges. On each lid is painted a quaint scene of a Dutch boy and girl.

"Let's kidnap Albert and set him free," Amanda suggests as they approach the brick and steel pen of the campus mascot, a six-foot-long alligator. The girls hang their heads over the points of the fence and examine the dull creature within. His heavy-lidded eyes are barely slits, his long, sculptured snout takes in air without a quiver. The zigzag points of his teeth lay at rest, sinister and ruthless-looking. Gleaming on the sharp angles of his back are a scattering of pennies, tossed there by bored students whose only purpose is to goad him into some sullen twitch. But nothing ever moves this prehistoric-looking animal, not heavy prods, not rocks, not even bricks. A splatter of blood-red paint gleams between his ears.

More often than not, when passing by his pen on her way to class, Francie sees his keeper working on the animal with paint remover and a stiff-bristled brush. (For these sessions, the alligator's jaw is tied shut with heavy rope.) Fraternity boys, at the height of their weekend drunkenness, think it a lark to dump a gallon of paint on Albert's head. Francie wishes that she and her friends could kidnap the alligator, carry him on their backs to the swamp, and set him free in some deep, green, silent spot under those gothic trees bowed down with Spanish moss.

"I think his eyes are sexy," Liz suggests, and they stare at Albert's eyes, dim and withdrawn under his armor, with the barest flicker of awareness in them.

"I get a chill," Amanda says, "thinking of how fast he could move, how that tail could flick around like lightning."

"I wonder how they mate," Liz says.

"And what they feel," Amanda adds.

"And if the earth moves."

They stare at the creature; they contemplate his inner life.

"I'm sure he hates living all alone in this little cell, on display all day and night, having to sit there while they dump paint on his head," Amanda remarks.

"Life is pain and suffering for all living creatures," Liz intones. "So why don't we try to forget the world's misery for a while, pretend that life is not a fool's futile errand, and go buy some yummy things to eat at the Piggly Wiggly?"

✳

"Don't look now, but guess who's coming!"

They glance demurely from under their lashes and see Professor Raskolnikov, their Russian lit teacher, coming swiftly along the path. Since they have discovered they are all in his class, they find him a ripe subject for discussion. His real name is full of guttural Russian syllables, nowhere near as pretty as he is, so they have given him this name of their choice. Now, as he comes toward them, his head is bent forward so that they can see the thick waves of his light brown hair. He is wearing his regulation tan loafers with thick, white crepe soles, so that he seems to bounce gracefully above the ground with each step.

More than once, Francie has heard him, after a particularly invigorating class, invite students to meet with him in the evening at the College Inn sandwich shop to continue their discussion of life and literature. Of course, only male students are invited. Girls can't go anywhere at night; they have strict curfews and must be locked up at an insanely early hour on weekdays. But sometimes, trapped in her dorm room on weeknights with Mary Ella and her bridal magazines, Francie imagines herself loose in the world, free to sit in a coffee shop till all hours, discussing ideas of the intellect, proposing solutions of importance, being free as a man.

Well, at least she is privileged to hear Professor Raskolnikov's theories in class, where his face is always illuminated, alive, his body as expressive as a dancer's as he gives some long, tender explication of a Chekhov story or a Tolstoy novel. For him and him alone, she will read a thousand-page Russian novel with patience. For him, she will tolerate Tolstoy's abuse of his wife, she will forgive Oblomov his century in bed, she will absolve the suffering, desperate (real) Raskolnikov of any and all of his crimes.

"Hello, Professor," Liz says, startling him out of his reverie, causing him to bring his head up and open his eyes, blinking as if shades have flown up and exposed him to bright sunlight.

"Oh, yes, yes, how are you all, my charming young ladies?" and he hurries along, coattails flapping, toward the bell tower.

"I wonder if he's married," Amanda muses, staring at his retreating back.

"Oh," Liz says slowly, "I don't think he's the marrying kind."

"You mean he just trifles with women?" Amanda asks.

"No, I don't mean that. I just think . . . I would guess he's not interested in women."

"What makes you say that? He's so handsome, I'd even call him beautiful. He has eyelashes like a girl, and even his face . . ."

"Exactly," Liz says.

"My God," Amanda stops on the path. "You don't think he's . . ."

"How would I know?" Liz says. "It's just a thought."

"How come you have such convoluted thoughts? That never would have occurred to me," Amanda complains.

Francie is thinking, with a kind of shock, that it never would have occurred to her, either. But suddenly it seems quite possible, even correct. To imagine Professor Raskolnikov this way swirls the picture around, changes the focus, alters the interpretation of his bouncy walk, his gleaming smile, his sensitive, passionate interpretations of the great Russian tales.

"You know," Francie says, "if we were men, we could meet with him in the evenings and discuss great literature."

"If we were men," Liz says, not unkindly, "we could meet with him for other reasons, other activities."

The three of them walk on, silent in their new imaginings.

✸

The Piggly Wiggly is downtown, four blocks from campus. At its entrance, they see strollers, children hanging onto their mothers' hands; they read signs on the door proclaiming: "Rib roast, 39 cents a pound."

Inside, a young Negro man is sweeping the floor with a wide broom where some glass has shattered in the aisle. He glances up, and Liz smiles at him. He lowers his head at once.

"You embarrassed him," Amanda whispers to Liz, after they've passed him by.

"I didn't mean to," Liz says. "I meant to smile at him, be friendly."

"You can't be friendly to them, not in the South."

"Soon they'll be in school with us," Liz says. "It's only fair. I hope it happens soon."

"I do, too," Francie says. She wants fairness everywhere. She wants the world to be fair to women, fair to Negroes, fair to everyone.

Amanda is looking at the aisles full of food. "I'm so tired of the dorms, dorm food," she sighs. "I wish we could cook some real food, in a real kitchen."

"Why don't we reserve the party kitchen, then?" Liz says, in her swift solving-problem tone. "It's early enough in the week to reserve it! We can cook in this weekend. We'll invite Bill, Bobby, and Jerry." She takes a wagon from a line of them and begins to walk along the aisles.

Francie is impressed by Liz's resolve, her decisiveness. Being able to make decisions fast (and with certainty, like a man) is an attribute to be desired.

"We'll have steak and baked potatoes and baby peas and a Caesar salad. . . ."

"Why don't you push the wagon, Francie?" Liz asks,

and Francie takes the helm, feeling grateful for a turn at wielding power, proud to feel some authority in a life that is essentially without any. Liz leads them to the jam and jelly section and studies the shelves. "Here it is!" she says gleefully, "Alvis jelly!" She pounces on a white jar that says on its label: "Dundee Orange Marmalade, Est. 1797."

"It's expensive," Amanda says. "Look at the price."

"Well, it's imported," Liz explains, "like so many fine products. Price should be no object when quality is the goal, remember that. This marmalade comes from England, so it's the best. The Alvis comes from England, and if Bill and the twins ever get that car fixed up and running, it will be worth a million."

Francie waits, leaning her arms on the cold metal of the cart, while Liz decides which jar is most beautiful. So the mystery is solved: the Alvis is a car. She was right to wait and not ask. In time she will know all.

✳

Now they are wending their way down a side street in the downtown section of Gainesville. The supermarkets and drugstores and restaurants are giving way to rundown wooden buildings and body shops with chain-link fences around them.

"Here it is," Liz says, and they walk up a long alley and around a corner. A sign over the open garage door says "THE GREASE MONKEYS"—and inside, wearing coveralls, is one of the beautiful twins. He's holding a long wrench in his hand, and his head is leaning deep under the hood of an oddly shaped white car. Inside, Francie can see the black coils of a motor.

"Anyone home?" Liz says.

At the sound of her voice, the twin emerges from the depths, coming up smiling. He continues beaming at Liz and then reduces his smile to a normal grim as he nods to the other girls.

"So where's The Boss?"

"Him and Bobby went out to get us some lunch," says the twin.

It smells in here of oil and dust, motors and metal. There is a sense of nothing soft, nothing clean, nothing inviting around. There is nowhere to sit. A pin-up girl from a *Playboy* magazine is mounted on a nail; Francie looks at it very fast, at the posed girl with satin skin and balloon breasts. She is wearing red, furry boots.

Amanda moves to stand closer to Francie. She whispers, "Look at the twin's face. Now imagine him with black hair. Wouldn't it be a miracle if Elvis Presley and these twins were really triplets? You know they say Elvis had a twin who died. But maybe he was really one of triplets and these twins are his brothers."

"I don't even know what Elvis looks like," Francie admits.

"The world considers him sexy," Amanda informs her. "That's the main thing."

Are the twins sexy? Francie considers this; they are very wonderful and amazing to look at, simply by virtue of the miracle of having the same face, body, and way of moving. But what is sexy? And can it be the same for Amanda, for Liz, and for Francie?

"So how is the Alvis coming?" Liz asks. The twin murmurs something in car language, about manifolds and carburetors, and Liz puts her arms around his waist and hugs him. "Just make it perfect and then sell it for a fortune. We're all counting on you to make us rich, you know."

"I'll do my best," the twin says, laughing shyly.

"Then we'll all adore you. I already do," Liz says. "Bill adores you. Liz and Francie also adore you."

"What about Bobby?" he asks dryly.

"Blood relatives never adore you," says Liz. "They're born to crucify you."

"Or you them," the twin says.

# 5

## Party Kitchen

Mary Ella Root watches Francie dress, step by step, for a Friday night out-of-room experience. There's no way around it; privacy is impossible here. Mary Ella stares, makes judgments, and passes comments from her crossed-leg guru position on her bed.

"Honey, no, I don't think that scarf goes with that sweater. I think maybe my little mother-of-pearl heart locket would be better, nestled right smack in the middle of your little chest."

"My little chest," Francie murmurs. She pulls out of her closet a white, heavy cotton, long-sleeved blouse, with buttons up to the neck, out to the wrists, a veritable coat of armor. This, and her gray wool straight skirt, with one small slit on the right side, is her absolute last choice. She can't go on rejecting herself much longer; she has to be down in the party kitchen in five minutes.

"Oh, honey, I'm so jealous you have a date," Mary Ella sighs. "I thought you and I were going to set a record, you know, the famous Dead-Duck Roommates who graduated from college without a single date."

"This isn't a date," Francie tells her for the fifth time. "We're just cooking downstairs for some friends of Amanda and Liz."

"But they're men, you said, right? Three men? And you're three women. I'll tell you, passion is inevitable. All closed up in that little room, all that steam from the stove, the aroma of garlic and onions, who knows what men will do. I hear that actual, total sex sometimes happens in that party kitchen," Mary Ella whispers. "The real thing. Couples who want privacy tape a piece of cardboard over that glass window in the door. You know which little window I mean?"

"We're not going to have sex," Francie assures her.

"I wonder how two people do it down there." Mary Ella hugs a stuffed kangaroo to her chest. "Maybe on the little table, or standing up. Maybe even on the stove once the burners have cooled down."

"Mary Ella! All we're going to do on that stove is cook steak! That's all!"

"Well, don't say I didn't warn you if things get out of hand. Once the beer gets to flowing, you never know."

"Apple juice is our beverage of choice, if that will set

your mind at ease. You know they don't allow alcohol in the dorms."

"Oh, let me dream on. But listen, hon, you really should wear a girdle."

"What for? I have nothing to gird."

"That's not the point, Francie. You're a girl. Girls have hips. You could borrow one of mine that's really teeny-tiny. I never could get it on. You need to wear it to be respectable. Over at Betty Lu's sorority house, the housemother smacks every girl on the bottom as she leaves to make sure she's wearing her girdle. Otherwise her jiggling could give the sorority a bad name."

"Don't you think that's weird?" Francie demands of her. "I mean, don't you ever stop and think how unnatural that is, to wrap yourself in elastic so tight you can't even breathe?"

"No, I do not think it's weird. I think it's necessary and moral. What's unfair is to incite men to their animal thoughts. And, frankly, since you want to know what I really think, I'll tell you. I think you're asking to be violated if you go down to the party kitchen not wearing a girdle."

"Oh please," Francie says. Her head is beginning to clang like an anvil. "I wish this evening were over with already. I wish I could stay in my bed and read."

"I'll go for you," Mary Ella offers. "Do you think anyone would know the difference?"

Swarming with crew-cut young men who have arrived to pick up their dates, the lobby is ablaze with noise and motion. Dozens of girls wearing hoop crinolines under their skirts crowd the front desk, three deep, as they wait in line to pull their sign-out cards and register their destinations. They jostle and bounce against one another like bumper cars.

Francie now faces a moral dilemma: is going to the party kitchen (which is down in the basement of the dorm) equivalent to going out, and thus does it require a sign-out? She will be in the building but won't be, technically, "at home." Perhaps this fact is crucial. Even more important is that she will be with companions of the male sex. Everyone knows that if men are involved, the ritual of sign-out is essential. The university has a right to know where the police should look for her body if she doesn't return by curfew.

Her sign-out card, made of posterboard, is nearly full. Across the top are the words: DATE, TIME, DESTI-NATION, NAME OF COMPANION, EXPECTED TIME OF RETURN, ACTUAL TIME OF RETURN. Over the months, Francie has created long elegant lines of "Des-tination: Library"—they skitter down the rows like dancing chorus girls.

Tonight she ponders: Name of companion? What if there is more than one? Expected time of return? What if she can't predict this with any accuracy? What if she never returns? As she privately debates with herself, she is elbowed by the gaggle of hooped and perfumed females. They are all anxious to get a head start on the night whose dreaded curfew threatens even as the evening begins.

Francie designates "Liz and Amanda" as her companions and puts a question mark at her expected time of return. Let them arrest her. Let them sue her. No one is permitted to sign in after midnight on weekends or ten on week nights; if a girl is late, she is formally campused and unable to leave her room for the next month of weekends. In fact, no girl can even get in the door after curfew; all entrances are locked and barred. The night watchman paces along the front porch like a sentry. People have reported that he pulls kissing, clinging couples apart bodily—sometimes violently—in order to get the girl in the door before the final bell.

Francie sighs. She places her card in the OUT section of the wooden box and backs away to let the flood of females surge forward.

At the far end of the lobby, a platoon of girls stand holding their arms out like tree branches. Hanging from them are the flags of their good luck, their boyfriends' shirts, which they have painstakingly ironed in their rooms, hung on wire hangers, and brought down to present to their dates as proof of their future uses and talents. The boys who have cars will lay these creaseless treasures over the front passenger seat in preparation for keeping them safe from what will happen later in the evening in the back seat.

No doubt at this very moment in the parking lot,

girls are climbing into the back seats of their boy-friends' cars for the ride to the movies or the frat house or the sock hop, committed to keeping one hand on the pastel pile of ironed shirts to protect them from wrinkles all the long way to their destination. (And later, Francie guesses, during whatever is happening in the back seat, their minds' eye will be on the main goal, keeping the shirts in the front seat wrinkle-free.)

Francie runs down the stairs to the basement to clear her head of the noise, the oppressive heat of the hormonal throng. On Friday nights, the dorm cafeteria downstairs is closed and silent. The metal legs of the orange vinyl chairs turned upside-down on the tables give off hard, cold gleams of light. There is a laundry room down here, a little shop that sells sanitary napkins and toothpaste and stamps, a storage area for trunks and suitcases, and the party kitchen.

This homelike arena—a mere kitchen—is kept locked and can be opened only by a key issued to a responsible applicant. Before this can occur, the applicant must submit a description (a minimum of two days in advance) of the activity to be performed therein, the number of guests who will accompany the applicant, the type of food that will be cooked ("list tentative menu"), and a deposit to cover possible damage to pots, dishes, silverware, or built-in appliances. A pledge must also be signed, swearing that "no untoward activities" will take place during the period contracted for and that, under no circumstances, will the glass window in the party kitchen be blocked "by natural or unnatural opaque substances."

(Last night Liz and Amanda took turns trying to guess what these substances might be. Was steam a natural substance? What about mashed potatoes, smeared over the glass?)

The dinner guests are already there! Francie hears laughter in the party kitchen, the clanking of silverware, the scraping of wooden drawers being slid on their runners. She peeks in the glass window and encounters a timeless domestic tableau: there in the frame of her vision are a man, a woman, a table laden with food. Pure essence of family life shines forth: from the kitchen she extrapolates a home with an upstairs and a downstairs. Upstairs, of course, would be the marital bedroom wherein may occur the longed-for act of conjunction. Upon the bit of glass before her, she envisions a screen full of throbbing amoebae extruding their parts, forming hooks and eyes, plugs and receptacles, arrows and quivers, hands and gloves, arms and sleeves, rings and fingers.

Francie screws her courage to the sticking point. She has a right to enter this kingdom of domestic bliss. Someday she will claim her place in such a kingdom. Though her knees are weak, she opens the door and enters with a sense of entitlement.

✳︎

The men seem to have an extraordinary interest in steak. They proclaim how long it's been since they've had "a big, juicy steak," how happy they are that these steaks are inch-thick Grade A Choice sirloin, dripping blood. The twins and Bill are gathered around the cutting board like surgeons around an operating table. Their eyes are fastened on Liz's graceful, competent hands as she trims off the excess fat with the dull serrated knife provided by the university. Francie stands there, on the edge of the action, as she stands everywhere: outside and waiting, waiting and wanting, wanting and wishing.

No wonder Mary Ella Root makes her life in bed. How much easier it is to stand back from the fray and refrain from pitching oneself into a contest one will surely lose, and only then after insults, affronts, rejections, and outright blows.

"Is there something I can do to help?" Francie asks.

Her voice surprises them. They didn't know she was there, had perhaps even forgotten she was coming.

Amanda hands her a bunch of paper napkins. "Sure, why don't you set the table?"

Liz adds, "Good idea, thanks, Francie." Thus— blessedly—they take her in, enlarge the circle to include her. She nearly cries with gratitude.

# 6

# Shellfish

Bill's eyes gleam with a devil glint. "Let's cover the glass window in the door," he proposes. "Let's see—how about we make a paste with flour and water? How about we use a few big lettuce leaves? Maybe we could just take Francie here and have her stand in front of the window all night. How about it, Francie?"

He's joking, of course he's joking. He winks at her to let her know he's a funny guy, a joker like her Jewish cousins who like to tease, to play practical jokes. He's like family to her. She knows this boy inside out. She shares his collective unconscious. He ought to be interested in her, she's from his tribe.

Yet he treats her like a little sister, a sidekick who's onto him. His real interest is in the blonde exotic Christian girl, the *shiksa,* the mysterious "other." Perhaps he's as mystified by Liz as Francie is mystified by the slow, southern machinations of the twins, by their nonverbal, side-by-side existence, by their almost psychic but unconscious communications with each other.

"So will you do it, Francie? Block the window so we can have our orgy in here? Or do you want to join the orgy? We can have Amanda block the window while we get you on the kitchen table!"

*Very funny.* Francie widens her eyes, lifts the corner of her lip slightly. *I understand you,* she indicates. *Watch out.*

The twins are busy shelling fresh shrimp, their contribution to the feast. As they peer through their eyeglasses, they take on an air of great concentration; again they look like little surgeons (or engineers), holding the curled creatures on the cutting board, pulling off their tails, cracking their shells, deveining their veins. Carefully they pull out the black, secret digestive material of each creature in one long thread.

"I won't eat any shrimp," Francie announces, though she's surprised to hear herself say it. "Jews don't eat shellfish." There, she has made the shocking statement, she has laid her cards on the table, indicated why she is by necessity different from these other two girls and why, she understands, she may in the end be ostracized.

"You're Jewish?" the twins say in unison. It's quite likely that, having grown up in Georgia, these boys have never actually met a Jewish person. She, in turn, has never seen a shrimp up close.

"I'm Jewish by birth," Francie says, "but the truth is I'm an atheist." There, she has done it again, shocked them, alienated herself. Burned her bridges.

"Hey, I'm an atheist, too," Bill says. "I'm trying to get Liz to join the club."

Liz clamps her lips shut. She won't joke about God.

"Why don't we start cooking this food?" Amanda suggests, all business. "We're allowed to be in the kitchen for a mere two hours. Let's get going here."

✶

The steaks broil, the shrimps curl up on their wooden skewers, turning from translucent to white. The salad is crisp, green, shiny with oil and vinegar. The rolls come out of the oven crackled and browned, the butter melts inside them in half a second.

They sit down to eat. They are all silent, chewing in an ecstasy of appreciation. The men saw away at their bloody steaks; the women prefer their steaks well done, the charred edges aromatic with blackened fat. They seem suspended in time, eating this one magnificent meal, sealed in a closed, private room, men and women scheduled and assigned to be together for two hours, in the heat of cooked food and of their young blood. Francie feels they are all captives in a gel-like medium, under a microscope, each of them oozing through it, gliding, sliding, feeling his power. Red meat and blood. Forbidden shellfish. Little green peas that slide and roll on the plate.

One pea rolls across the table and down into the lap

of the twin beside Francie. It bounces over his belt and lodges in the fly of his pants.

He pokes it out, he blushes, he laughs. Francie sees the delicate stubble of a day's growth of beard on his fair skin, on his slightly freckled skin. Which twin is he, sitting beside her, his arm within an inch of hers on the table?

Is he Bobby? Jerry? She simply can't tell. It hardly matters. The way they place their long legs at wide angles in front of them under the table makes her want to step in between the angles and fit herself in. She feels herself in an underwater wave, an anemone waving wherever the tide takes her. Wash me up against him, either this twin or that one. She is amazed at her unwilled promiscuous instinct. Each time she feels it, it's stronger. Soon it may overtake her.

✳

Time for dessert. Amanda and Liz, proper southern belles, rise from the table to get the ice cream from the freezer and dish peach-apricot sundaes into six small bowls. They set out the spoons with delicate silver clinks. They distribute small flowered napkins, acting as perfectly proper immaculate little housewives doing their duty.

Francie lolls in a drowsy heat, letting them serve. Her veins must surely be full of intoxicating brew, except that she has drunk only apple juice, as innocent as the fruit on the tree.

They eat all the ice cream, licking their spoons.

"Listen," Bill says, leaning his head forward, eyeing them one by one. "I think we ought to do this all the time."

"You can only rent the party kitchen twice a semester," Amanda recites from the rule sheet. "And," she adds, like a little schoolteacher, "we must be certain to leave the surfaces immaculate and dry, the stove-top free of grease, the broiler pan cleaned and in the drain rack on the sink." Her glimmering blonde curls vibrate with emphasis as she speaks: "Count the utensils; be sure nothing is thrown into the trash or removed by accident."

"I say let's all live together!" Bill whispers, the devil's dart gleams red in his eye.

"Oh, sure," says one of the twins, the one beside Francie. He laughs low, a tone between a growl and a purr. "And let's all fly to the moon."

"That will happen in time," Bill assures them. "But I'm totally serious. Why not? Next term we *could* all live together off campus. We're all seniors, and seniors have Privilege. You girls can finally get out of this jail of a dorm. We'll find some old house to rent, and we can cook together, and we'll have none of this bullshit about curfews and party kitchen rules."

"What would we tell our parents?" Amanda says, her face red with excitement.

"Who says you have to tell them?" Bill tells her. "You tell them you're sharing a place with Liz and Francie. Don't you know about white lies?"

"I don't lie," Amanda states unequivocally.

"Then start," says Bill.

He looks at Francie. "You lie," he says. "Am I right?"

"Sometimes," she admits, "I have to."

"I knew you were a smart cookie," he says. "You'll come and join in the plan with us, won't you?" Bill gets up from his chair and comes to stand behind her. He puts his hands on her shoulders. He presses down on them. She isn't used to casual contact from men; his hands feel monumental, intimate, thrilling. She's confused. She looks over at Liz, who is watching them carefully.

"Maybe," she says. Maybe to everything, to living in a house with men, to being a smart cookie, to lying, to wanting to be touched again, by Bill, by a twin, by any man at all. "I think it would be interesting to consider."

"Then consider it." Bill commands her, letting her go.

The twins eyes are fused across the table. Then the six of them look around at one another. They all begin to smile.

Some pact has been sealed, here among the slippery green peas and in the heavy aroma of animal blood. Here at their party in the party kitchen, they have come to an understanding.

# 7

# Panty Raid

"Throw 'em down!"

"Throw 'em down!"

"Throw 'em down!"

The roar of men's voices rises up from the street like a geyser, falling away, then shooting upward with new intensity.

"Okay. Throw 'em down, Francie. Let's give the little boys what they want."

"Throw what?" Francie asks from the floor of Liz's room, where she sits leaning against the bed, reading, having come up here from her room to study.

"Throw 'em down my panties," Liz says, reaching back an arm to pull open her dresser drawer without even lifting her eyes from the pages of her book. Feeling around, she plucks out a pair of red lace panties and tosses them over to Francie.

"Go on, toss them out the window. Give those sweet Florida farm boys a little thrill. You know how boys are, Francie, at this age, with their hot little hormones. You know they don't have any self-control; they can't help themselves. You know what they say, don't you? If they don't get it, their balls turn blue."

Something must be going on with Liz; Francie hears an undercurrent of anger that's got a new, bitter edge to it. Liz has never, till now, been less than ladylike. Outside the dorm windows, the rigorous chant that has been gaining in volume and power during the last minutes is rising to a climactic clamor.

"Throw 'em down! Throw 'em down!" The voices are deep, surprisingly in tune: a boys' church choir grown up. Francie pictures the moist red lips of the men, their earnest, needy faces upturned to the windows of the cloistered women.

"You're not serious, Liz. You must be kidding, aren't you?"

Liz is reading again, with perfect concentration. In her sheer white baby doll pajamas, she looks about eight years old. The coil of her crook-necked lamp flares on the desk like a cobra, its hooded head sending out an aura of light around her yellow hair.

"They got needs, honey," Liz says, sounding almost like Mary Ella Root. "You know needs? Nature has got its requirements, sweetheart, and you can't go against nature."

Francie examines the lace panties, feeling the scratchy edge of the organdy trim against her fingertips.

"They sound dangerous, down there."

"All men are dangerous, Francie. It's in the nature of the animal."

"Even Bill?"

"Bill is the most dangerous. The sweetest ones, the cleverest ones, they catch you unaware."

Just then Amanda pushes open the door of the room and comes in, carrying a portable typewriter. "My ribbon is faded, so I had to borrow this from Lorlene to write my paper. I asked her, 'Are you sure you don't want to keep this here in case you need a weapon if the men get in and you need to throw something at them?' And do you know what she said? She said, 'Let them have me. It's time. I'm withering on the vine!' Can you imagine?"

"Aren't we all?" Liz remarks dryly. "In Samoa, the native girls have intercourse at thirteen. Maybe eleven. Some even at nine."

Amanda ignores this remark and goes to the window, where she peeks out between the slit in the curtains. "God! There are so many of them out there! It looks like all the fraternities are down on the lawn, and the football team, too."

"Relax your little soul," Liz says. "They'll get tired. They'll get it all out of their systems and go home soon."

"I'm scared," Amanda says. "If they did get in, it wouldn't be a joke. What about you, Francie? Are you scared?"

"A little. They do sound ominous."

"If we lived off campus next term," Liz says, "we could avoid all this. They never have panty raids at those big houses in the old part of town. They don't have room checks and night watchmen and sign-out cards. . . ."

"Maybe the three of us could rent a place," Amanda ventures.

"No! That's not what I'm thinking. You know what I'm thinking. Bill is after me every day, that's all he talks about now, but you know I can't do it without the two of you. If the six of us lived together, it would be much cheaper, and much safer, too, with our built in bodyguards—those strong, handsome, well-built twins, and my wily, sly Bill."

"We could never . . ."Amanda says.

"And we could all go to the Piggly Wiggly once a week to shop, and then cook magnificent meals, like the one we had in the party kitchen. We could do that every night." Liz doesn't look at them as she proposes this because of the astonishing thing she is really suggesting: that the three of them, unmarried good girls, live—unsupervised—with men. Francie knows why Liz can't look them in the eye. She can't look up either, because of what she knows might show in her own face.

Liz rises from her desk and goes to the window sill, where she begins to rotate the handle to open the window.

"Don't open that!" Amanda insists. "You know the rules in case of a panty raid: stay away from the windows, keep them locked, and keep the curtains drawn. If a break-in occurs, barricade your door with heavy furniture."

"Yes, yes—'Under no circumstances venture into the hall.' Damn rules!" Liz snaps. "Don't dictate rules to me, please! This is my fourth year of rules."

She flings open the curtains and stands looking down. When she leans forward, the soft, pale backs of her thighs shine with downy golden hairs. No wonder men want to get into the building. How beautiful we women are, Francie thinks. Even me. She could almost fall in love with Liz herself. Does that mean she isn't normal? That's she's attracted to women? She hopes not, but who knows about these things?

Amanda rushes to the wall to snap off the light switch. "Liz, they might be able to see in. They might see everything." Then, once the room is safely dark, Amanda says, "If we six lived together, how could we ever tell our parents the truth?"

"Forget truth," Liz says over her shoulder. "Either you choose 'tell-the-truth-to-parents' or you have a life. Take your pick. Now put the light back on, Amanda. Do it!" she commands.

When the light comes on, they see that Liz has

pulled off the top of her pajamas and is standing bare-breasted, facing out, framed in the window.

"Liz! Don't!"

Liz takes a few steps back to retrieve the red lace panties from Francie, who is still holding them. Then she goes back to the window, planting her palms against the glass.

"Oh, don't!" Amanda begs.

With a quick motion, Liz flips the levers that unlock the screen, top and bottom. She brings the screen into the room and then leans out. She waves. She yells something about "boys" or "balls," and then she tosses her panties down to the men.

Francie pictures the little nylon flame, wafting slowly down, like a red flag flying into a crowd of bulls. A roar comes up from below. The three of them crowd against the window, watching the pandemonium below, the wild contest among men who are battling one another for the prize.

"You're really crazy," Amanda accuses Liz. "Now we'll be campused forever, if they find out whose room those came from." Her eyes are full of panic as she glances around the room. Then, beginning to whimper, she shoves her desk across the floor, toward the door. They can hear screams coming from all around, from up and down the halls, from the rooms above and below them.

Francie, still at the window, can see lights coming on in all the rooms of the brick fortress of Broward

Hall, sees other windows opening all across the quad, sees girls in their nightgowns doing cheesecake poses and belly dances behind their glass windows. A rain of silken parachutes begins fluttering down in the wind, hundreds of lace panties, in all colors of the rainbow.

"God, we're dead ducks," Amanda moans in terror. "There's no turning back now."

✳

They see the siege begin upon Broward Hall. The first offensive line storms the paltry defense of the lone security guard on the front porch of the dorm, and, in no time, the lobby has been penetrated by an army of drunk, ecstatic college boys. Because their room is at the end of a wing, Liz, Francie, and Amanda can see what's happening through the windows of the lobby. The men are streaming in the door and going every which way. They leap over the reception desk, they toss the sign-out cards in the air, they fling letters from the open mailboxes, they pillage the bulletin boards—all the while hooting and howling.

The girls watch till they can stand no longer stand on their feet. Liz collapses on her bed. Amanda stations herself on top of the desk she's moved against the door, pressing her ear against it to see if the men have made it up to the fourth floor.

"One year," Amanda informs them, "they say a man did get in and carried off a girl slung over his shoulder like a sack of beans."

"Well, I would guess she didn't get in by curfew. I wonder how they punished her," Liz says in a deadly still voice.

✳

Hours later, after city firemen and policemen have joined the campus security forces to put to rout the mob of men, after the halls have stopped reverberating with the thunderous noise of boots and shouts and scuffles, after the paddy wagons have made off with the rowdiest and most inebriated offenders, and after the main desk has buzzed each room to announce that the building is secure once again, Liz and Amanda cautiously push away the furniture with which they have barricaded the door and let Francie out.

The hall is a shambles. Empty beer cans and bottles are scattered about like spent ammunition; the top of a wastebasket has been pulled off in order that some fraternity boy could vomit into it. At the public phone at the end of the hall, there is a line of girls, waiting to call home—to assure their parents that they have not been raped or killed or carried off—before news of the panty raid hits the newspapers tomorrow morning.

On her way back to her room, Francie sees girls walking about like shell-shocked soldiers. A number are dazed, wild-eyed, others are fully dressed in sweaters and winter coats, some are still in their nightgowns and hair curlers. One of them stops Francie and says, "I heard that a girl on the first floor was attacked. Do you know if it's true?" Francie shakes her head. "And another girl was climbing out a window to meet her boyfriend and she fell. The ambulance took her away; she might have broken her back."

So. This thrilling night will have consequences. This night is not just about the beauty, youth, and desirability of young women; nor is it only about the strength, desire, and power of young men.

When Francie reaches her room, a girl named Nina from across the hall says, "Mary Ella came rushing out of her room to look for you just as the men got in. They rampaged right over her. She fell, and Mrs. Taylor found her on the floor, hysterical. She had one of the security people take her to the hospital to be checked to be sure she's still intact."

"Was there any doubt?"

"Well, Mary Ella could hardly speak. She kept saying she didn't know what had happened." The girl makes a strange face. "I think it if had happened to me, if some man had raped me, I'd remember. Wouldn't you, Francie?"

# 8

# Fluff

rofessor Raskolnikov circles his classroom desk as he speaks, keeping his eye on the cup of coffee steaming at its center. A shimmery bit of glazed doughnut is clinging to the edge of his lip. From time to time, as he lectures, he stops to take another bite of his doughnut.

"Forgive me, a busy morning, you must excuse me, there's never enough time to get organized, is there?"

Francie keeps her eye on the doughnut; it lies temptingly on the plate, its sugary sheen making her mouth water. She's already had two for her breakfast this morning, though her father's main advice about college was that she must be sure to eat scrambled eggs every day. She can't do it; she opens her eyes each morning with a real hunger, a desperate longing to feel the soft plunge of her teeth into a cushion of tender, iced, fragrant, fried dough. Doing what is good for her as opposed to doing what she longs to do is surely one of the major battles of her life. A bit of verse her father used to recite comes to Francie's mind:

*As you wander on through life, brother,*
*Whatever be your goal,*
*Keep your eye upon the doughnut*
*And not upon the hole*

Across the room, Liz and Amanda are sitting attentively, like good students, with their pens poised over their notebooks. So far, Professor Raskolnikov has said nothing a student might record. He seems distracted, bouncing about on his crepe soles and running his fingers through his wavy hair.

"Plots," he says. "Do you think that what makes a great novel is its plot, or do you think what makes it great is its degree of anguish? Does enough anguish experienced by the characters of a novel make a plot? Or must we have events? Must an author move a character from A to B, have him abandon C, kill D, and marry E? Or is it enough for an author merely to climb inside one character's head and sit there, look around, and tell us what he sees? As we all know, no person ever lives in any head but his own. Not even for one second in an entire lifetime. We never, ever can know what another human being's life is like. Even in the throes of great passion; even at moments of deepest intimacy. We are forever locked right inside here, for all eternity." He taps several times, rather hard, on his skull, takes a fast bite of doughnut, a fast sip of coffee, then goes to the blackboard and writes—in huge, wild letters—the word FLUFF.

"Copy this down," he says, and Francie dutifully adjusts her pen, writes down the word. For some reason, the other students are writing away, writing on and on—but why? What could they be doing? There's only one word up there. In a matter as simple as this, Professor Raskolnikov has demonstrated his belief— what motivates another person is a total mystery to her. Francie no more understands anyone else than she understands a clump of Spanish moss.

Now her professor writes, under the word FLUFF:

F = Friction
L = Love
U = Unfaithfulness
F = Forgiveness
F = Forever After

"There," he says. "Tell that story from the mind of your hero or heroine and you have the combination that will make a great novel. Remember that and you know all there is to know about literature. Class dismissed."

And he's gone out the door. Is he really gone? He has left his doughnut and coffee on the desk. He must be kidding. They have been in class only ten minutes. Francie looks around the room. Everyone is looking at everyone else. Francie checks her assignment sheet.

Today they were to have discussed Turgenev's *The Father*. Where has her professor gone? To the men's room? Will he be back? Is this some kind of a test?

She smoothes her skirt; she glances across the room at Liz, who raises her eyebrows and makes a strange face. A low buzzing begins; students are leaning across the aisles, whispering to one another. A few begin to gather up their books. What is there to do now? She has almost an hour till her next class.

Francie knocks her pen off the desk; the boy sitting next to her dives to retrieve it. When he hands it back, he smiles, and keeps smiling at her. He's a generic student—the crew-cut, the sweater, the flat forehead, the pug nose, the nicely shaped chin. There's something flavorless about him: she guesses he's in the right fraternity, the right service club, on a sports team. But he's looking at her in a certain way, turning toward the aisle to face her. She feels her heart sink as he cracks his knuckles; she knows what's coming. He will ask her to go out for coffee. She is witnessing the electrical signals that precede an approach. She has seen it happen often enough, and now it's coming her way.

Why does she feel like crying? How can it ever happen in the right way for *her*? Will it ever come together—the right boy, the right feeling, the right time, circumstance, need, opportunity? Francie can't imagine that it ever could—the odds are totally against it. But then who are all these paired people she sees together, everywhere—on campus paths, on line at the movies, eating together at the Gator Grill, kissing good-night on the porch of Broward Hall every night of the week?

Perhaps she was born without some essential element: the hook to find a mate. Where is it attached on her? How would she use it if she were to locate it? Even though it's invisible, without it she is surely a handicapped person.

"Frances, right?" the boy begins (he is reading her name from the cover of her notebook).

"Francie," she corrects him.

"So—what do you think of these Russian novels. Pretty long, huh?"

"Some are."

"And those names! Who can keep them straight?"

"Sometimes it's difficult."

"So listen, Frances, would you be willing to tell me what the hell is going on in this novel?" He waves his copy of *The Father*. "I mean, if I don't pass this course, I'm done for. So since we're not having class today, how about if you have time—could we sit outside for a few minutes and you fill me in?"

She's relieved. She's furious.

"Sure. Okay, why not?" Other students are leaving now; Professor Raskolnikov is apparently gone for good. Francie says to the boy, "What's your name?"

"Clendon Hudson."

"Come on, Clendon," she tells him. "I'll try to straighten it out for you."

Liz and Amanda follow her with their eyes as she walks out of class with the boy. So it's worth something to be followed by a male, to have him reach ahead of her to hold the door open. But Francie is falling apart inside. Hinges are coming loose. She thinks she might just keel over in despair. Something has to change soon. Something has to happen or she'll be smack in the middle of her life and it won't be a life. She'll soon be teaching second grade and making collages out of straws and bottle caps. That's what young women do if they don't marry. She'll live and die without drama. Without Friction, Love, Unfaithfulness, Forgiveness, and Forever After.

"Let's sit here," she says to Clendon as they pass a vacant bench in front of the library. "Now here's the secret of how you can pass this course. The main thing to remember is that Russian literature is about pain and suffering. Anguish—that's really all you need to know. *Anguish, torment and misery.*"

"No kidding," he says. "And I thought it was about deep stuff."

# 9

# Sermon

When Francie asks Mary Ella Root for permission to borrow one of her girdles, Mary Ella's mouth falls open. Francie can see the pink bubble gum hanging off her roommate's upper palate like an upside-down marsupial, something bare and vulnerable.

"Honey, whatever for? You're just a rack of bones. You told me yourself, there's no hips on you anywhere to hold in." Mary Ella looks puzzled, as she often does these days. She seems to have lost track of the flow of time. Since the night of the panty raid, she has barely left the room, even for classes. She's deeper in hibernation than her usual patterns require. When one of her professors sent an inquiry about her absence to the dean, who sent one to the dorm, Mrs. Taylor came to the room to inquire. In her fierce defense, Mary Ella drew herself up to full dirigible size and made it clear: "Those heavy-breathing men breaking in here sent a major shock to my delicate system, and the only sensible thing to do is stay in the bed and get healthy again. I'll know when it's time to come out. Don't you worry about me."

"Just tell me where you keep the girdle and I'll get it myself," Francie asks. "You always urge me to wear one." She breathes deeply and readies herself for the plunge. She knows breaking the news to Mary Ella this way is underhanded, but she hasn't figured out an approach that's any kinder or that will save her from giving the cruel blow.

"The reason I need to borrow your girdle is that I need to look extra-respectable when I go with Liz and Amanda to find a place to rent off campus for next term."

"Off campus! Oh, Lordy, save me! Don't tell me you're going to leave me, Francie. Are you? If you say yes, I'll die right here this minute."

"Oh, Mary Ella! It's not that I want to leave you, or even move away from you," Francie begins, "but the truth is I just can't live in the dorms forever. I'm almost done with college and I need a little freedom from janitors yelling 'man-in-the-hall' at the top of their lungs and Mrs. Taylor checking our bra straps when we come in to see if they're twisted or mussed up. I need to be able to breathe!"

"I knew it," Mary Ella says. "Those fourth floor

Bobbsy twins got their claws into you, those little blond nose-in-the-air stuckups."

"Be fair, Mary Ella. Liz and Amanda are really nice girls."

"They think they're God's gift," Mary Ella says. "It's just dumb luck, you know, that those two were born thin as gate posts and with perfect skin. But don't I have a lot to offer you, too, Francie? Don't I give you devotion? Don't I give you good advice? I would give you not only my girdle to wear but any piece of my jewelry, including my ankle bracelet with the five gold hearts and three Cupids; I would give you even the most intimate garment of apparel I own! Honey, you know I can't manage without you. You're my sandbag in the flood. Who knows what I'll get next? They might move some girl in here with low morals! Who snores! Who would use my best nail polish without asking."

"Please, Mary Ella—don't make me feel so guilty. I think I might actually go mad if I don't get a change from sign-out cards and emergency hall meetings. How the guard goes around to each couch where a couple is sitting and says, 'Remember, all four feet on the floor at all times.' Do you think it's right that girls should be treated like criminals? Do you?"

Francie walks over to where she has thumbtacked to the side of the closet the "Women Students' Regulations." She flips the pages.

"Let me read you this, Mary Ella, and tell me if you think this is fair: '*Men Guests may not, except under extraordinary circumstances and only with express permission of the housemother, be received in the rooms. This regulation applies to fathers, brothers, and any male relatives.'* Mary Ella, when my father wanted to carry my trunk into my room last fall, he wasn't allowed to go past the lobby! Do you think that's a decent rule? And what about this one:

*'Shorts, slacks, pedal pushers, or dungarees are not to be worn in the public areas, including lobbies, lounges, porches, grounds, University buildings, or any places accessible to visitors EXCEPT when picking up mail or packages in the halls OR when engaged in sports, provided skirts or NONTRANSPARENT coats are worn when going to and from the sports area.'*

"Doesn't that make you furious? Why would they assume that any girl would intend to wear a see-through raincoat over her lacy underwear in order to show everything she has to the boys? I'm so tired of this, Mary Ella. I need to be trusted. I need some freedom."

"Maybe whoever made those rules knows the truth about human nature," Mary Ella says mournfully.

"Well, maybe I don't think human nature is as sinful as the authorities think it is. All this keeping-out of men is what starts these panty raids. Any time you forbid a person to do something is when they decide they absolutely have to do it. That panty raid was a very scary thing, don't you think?"

"Scary? Baby doll, I nearly kissed myself good-bye when I heard those bulls snorting down the hall. I knew you were out there somewhere, all alone, wandering in the halls, maybe trying to get back to our room, so I just went out to find you—"

"That was really brave and good of you, Mary Ella. I really, truly do thank you."

"Of course, I didn't know I would pass right out from fright. But I did it because I love you, sweetheart. I was going to save your honor with my last breath."

"But Mary Ella, what is my honor? Do you mean my virginity? And—is a girl's virginity so important?"

"Well, of course! What's more important? What's a girl without her honor? She's a lost soul. She's a ruined vessel."

"So they like to tell us," Francie says. "But sometimes I wonder."

"Don't wonder! Don't even think that! You could fling your eternal soul into Hell just imagining it."

"Okay. Let's not imagine any further. Are you still willing to let me wear your girdle?"

"Francie, love," Mary Ella's eyes are soulful, almost tearful. "What would you say to this idea? Maybe I could move in with you and your two skinny little girlfriends. Maybe I could get to like them."

"Move in with us?"

Mary Ella nods, the little pouch of flesh under her chin shaking earnestly.

Francie doesn't know what she can say. She blurts out, fast, the one truth that might save her. "But Mary Ella—we're planning to live with *men*!"

"No!"

"Yes, really."

"God, are you listening?" She cups her hands like a megaphone and shouts toward the ceiling. "Tell me I didn't really hear her say that!"

"Listen, Mary Ella. The plan is that we're hoping to find a big old house to rent and share it with these three nice guys that Liz knows, two of them are twins, and they all run a little business in town, a garage where they fix foreign cars. It would be really cheap for all of us to share a place that way—"

"That is *absolutely* immoral, Francie."

"No, it's just convenient."

"It's a sin. Pure and simple."

"But we're not going to be . . ."

"It doesn't matter. It's forbidden. Only in the holy bonds of matrimony is cohabiting allowed, and for good reason."

"We wouldn't be cohabiting, not. . . ."

"You never know! Temptation blinds a person!" Mary Ella grabs her bed pillow and crushes it to her breast. "Even I could be tempted, did you know that? Never mind! Count me out, Francie. And consider me grateful that I don't have to share this room with a loose woman next term. Take my girdle if you still want it; it's in the second drawer there, on the left. And if you take it, you keep it. I definitely don't want it back. And I can't tell you how disappointed I am in you."

"I'm sorry you feel that way."

"How else could I feel?"

There is no answer to that. Like the fallen woman she is, Francie struggles into the girdle in full view of Mary Ella's judging eyes. She tugs the pink elastic thing on with wild, hip-wrenching wiggles, fearing she is spraining the muscles in her upper arms and dislocating her spinal column. The little garter tabs jingle like bells. Now she has to pull on stockings, as well. She is sweating like an animal on the slaughter block.

Mary Ella watches like an angry Buddha from the bed, her eyes red as coals. As Francie finally succeeds in dressing herself, as she picks up her basket bag and goes to the door, Mary Ella says, "It breaks my heart to think about the misery that's coming to you. And you know? Anyone seeing you on the street would think you're just a decent, pure-minded, respectable girl."

# 10

# Letter Home (1)

*D*ear Mom and Dad:

    *You will be happy to hear that I have been asked to live off campus this second term of our senior year with my friends Liz and Amanda, whom I have gotten to know quite well in the dorms recently. We are going to move this weekend into the big house of Liz's French professor, who is away on sabbatical in France. He is charging us practically nothing, since he is more than happy to have some reliable people living in his house, watering his plants, and making sure that things are taken care of. We are thrilled that we will finally be able to have some home-cooked food (and save a fortune on cafeteria bills).*

    *Liz and Amanda are really very fine girls; both of them are in childhood education and are very good students. Like me, they are interested in literary and cultural events, and we do many interesting things together.*

*Some friends of theirs are helping us to move, so don't worry that I'll be carrying my trunk by myself.*

*My schoolwork is going very well, and every day provides me with exciting and educational experiences. I am happy and grateful to be the first person in our family who will graduate from college (and if I want to graduate I'd better get back to my books!) You know that I am always aware of the sacrifices you are making to keep me in school, and I hope I can make you proud of me.*

*Love you all very much, Francie*

Even as she is mailing this stilted fiction home, Francie is thinking of what she will tell her parents in the next pep rally of assurance. Above all, she considers it her duty to regale her mother and father with news of how busy, happy, productive, popular, and carefree she is.

In the meantime, she is in utter despair about her future. A few more months and she will be out of school—and then what? Go home to live with her parents? Get a job as a ticket-taker in the local movie house?

Sometimes she imagines herself taking up the bohemian life, in the manner of Reginald and Lulu—perhaps moving to Greenwich Village in New York and writing a great novel. She yearns to be a writer, not as magnificent as Tolstoy, of course, but a fine writer, one who tells the truth about life in the most passionate and honest way.

Now and then, as she sits daydreaming in the library or studying on the grass near the bell tower, she imagines a scene that excites her soul: in it she has carried her portable typewriter into the woods and set it up on a tree trunk, and there, lost in writing great thoughts, she is discovered, at last, by the man she will love. This handsome young man comes upon her as she is typing intently, immersed in creating truth and beauty, creating a masterpiece of ageless literature. He taps her on the shoulder; she turns around and finds that the miracle has happened: Cupid's arrow has pierced both her heart and his.

In this fantasy worthy of Mary Ella, the handsome young man, the proverbial Prince, falls helplessly in love with her and is astonished and impressed by her selfless dedication to Art, and together they ride off on his white steed.

Either that, or he will ask her out for a beer.

✗

Beer and cigarettes. Francie dislikes the sour pungent aroma of beer. Cigarettes and the choking haze they emit are an even greater mystery. Students passing out tiny rectangular boxes containing four cigarettes stand on campus paths offering the free samples to everyone who passes by. Francie has a dozen of these boxes in her dresser drawer, though she's not sure why she keeps them. Sometimes she sniffs a box and recoils from the sharp, wild smell of shredded tobacco. If beer and cigarettes, which are universally worshipped by the general student body, are so odious to her, how then would she feel about sexual intercourse, which stands high (possibly highest) on the list of student pleasures?

Who is having it? Not one girl on campus and every one of the boys, from the looks of things. And where are they having it? In cars, when possible. At a few squalid off-campus apartments. In the married-student dorms, known as FlaVets, where sex is legal, but only veterans on the GI bill and their families are allowed to live there.

Some students go to the Devil's Millhop, a sinkhole deep in the woods, which is a famous site for wild parties. Francie has heard rumors that the science labs are used in off-hours, that some professors give students keys to their offices in which to study (but the desk is used for less intellectual purposes). Even the alligator pen, it has been reported, is used by the drunkest of celebrants who are so inebriated that they willingly hop in with Albert the Alligator and the girl of their choice.

Can it be true that the infamous act of love may forever evade Francie?

She desires not merely the act but the lifelong exquisite consequences, the sublime results of true love. (Is she as besotted as Mary Ella by these clichés? Isn't she tougher than that?)

For several weeks now, Francie has been observing a girl who lives in the dorm and her beloved. Whenever Francie passes through the lobby or comes in from the library at curfew, she sees them together in the dorm lounge peering into each other's eyes—it seems they do this for hours on end. They are quiet, polite, and discreet and are always careful to observe the rule of "four feet on the floor at all times." At the sound of the curfew bell, however, they cling to each other with the desperation of two going down on a sinking ship. Before the young man is finally ousted by the security guard, sometimes bodily, the couple visibly suffer the utter violence of separation. Wrested from her beloved, the girl walks up the ramp to her room each night with tears in her eyes, her shoulders shaking with sobs.

To think that two people could worship and cherish one another with such intimacy, tenderness, and heated conspiracy! Envy sends an icy shiver up Francie's spine each time she sees them enact this ritual parting. How on earth will she ever hope to find such beauty, such passion?

She is quite sure by now that she will be forever on the outside, watching life taking place beyond her. She pictures one of those souvenir crystal paperweights with a house inside the glass dome, with a fluttering of snowflakes falling softly, softly falling upon its sloping rooftop. The windows of the love nest are lit, the fire is cozy, the bedroom is dark and private.

Francie doesn't even see herself outside the house in the snow. She's looking in from a distance beyond the magical circle, far beyond the boundaries of the crystal ball, lost in the deep dark woods of loneliness, forever and permanently outside possibility.

# 11

# Playing House

Here they all are: three men and three women together, having dinner in their new house. On this night, the main dish is one-half of an iceberg lettuce apiece. Liz has a theory that eating greens will make them healthy and give them long life. In preparation, she has chilled three large heads of lettuce, sliced them fiercely in half with a silver cleaver, and served them—("Lettuce on a bed of lettuce," she points out)—ice-cold crunchy, with lots of salt.

The six of them sit around the large battered oak dining table, chewing seriously like ruminants, lettuce leaves hanging out of their mouths.

After dinner, the twins go back to what they have been doing all afternoon, drafting engineering designs on their identical drawing boards set up at one end of the living room. They seem to be designing whatever engineering students will have to design later in life. Francie glances at their work and understands none of it; she sees large sheets of paper on which are drawn lines with angles and numbers and degrees and measurements. The work is parched-looking, empty of curves and colors. Each twin from time to time looks up something in identical copies of a textbook titled *Strength of Materials*.

The twins, as they work, are themselves—by contrast—a design of subdued curves and colors. They have intense round blue eyes and dark arched eyebrows. They wear orange and brown argyle socks and iridescent eyeglass frames. They remind Francie of a strange species of bird she once saw in a zoo, birds that moved on hinged long legs and ducked their heads in private signals to one another, paced in repetitive patterns around their cage, and kept a certain, but definite, distance from one another's bodies. The twins echo these movements, communicating without words, exchanging information by grunts and elbow movements, as when they want to indicate that *Gunsmoke* is about to come on TV or when it's time to break out the carton of peppermint stick/vanilla ice cream.

In this large, cluttered house, each of them has arranged to have his own bedroom, although Liz and Bill are often closeted together in one or the other of their rooms. When the two of them are hidden away from the others, no one refers to their absence. When they finally come out, joining the others casually, no one looks directly at them, nor do they glance into anyone's faces. The twins generally keep their attention on whatever homework or TV show absorbs them at the moment, and Amanda and Francie just wait. For a long time— once they are all in the same room—no one can think of anything to say. Finally, someone asks a question or passes around some pretzels, and the dangerous, imaginative tension breaks down. Then they can all breathe again.

*Living with men! Living with men!* sings the refrain in Francie's mind. Is this sin? Will God strike her dead? From what she knows of God in the Old Testament and from her History of Religion class, this God is a very angry, demanding sort, full of ideas of revenge and punishment. He seems, moreover, contentious, goading, enjoys asking for outrageous sacrifices, sets up dares no one can win, strikes down dead those who don't please him, and—in general—uses his special powers to produce weapons of nature no one else can muster: plagues, droughts, floods and pestilence.

Francie, even in her childhood, never made God's acquaintance personally, nor has she ever had a transcendent revelation through a personal miracle. She pretty much can do without God. Amanda and Liz, on the other hand, have had intensive and early acquaintance with God's requirements, having been dragged to church from infancy. Whether or not they are actively involved with him at the moment, they definitely seem to acknowledge the existence of a lifelong bond ready to be reactivated at a time of their choosing.

Francie can't imagine God as being God-the-Father (her own father is never bossy, never punishes her, never raises his voice). She imagines God in relation to herself, when she tries to imagine him at all, as being rather like one of the football players on campus who's never given her a glance and who dates only cheerleaders. Should somehow he meet Francie, he'd know at once he has no use for her because she is not going to adore him or put his will before her own.

Never mind sin. As far as her immortal soul is involved, she's just sharing a big old house with some students. She glances around the room; Amanda sits studying in the wicker armchair, pulling little shreds of wicker off the armrest with her fingers. Liz and Bill are reading, at opposite ends of the long couch, each under a separate pool of light from their reading lamps.

Francie makes her unremarkable proposition. "Anyone want to help me with the dishes?"

✳

In the two weeks they've lived here, they've developed a nightly ritual. Usually Liz and Bill, with the help of Amanda and Francie, prepare the dinner. After dinner, Francie calls the twins to action.

Tonight, as on the other nights, the twins rise

and step back from their drafting tables and stretch (they are like those strange lanky birds extending their wings, craning their necks) and follow Francie into the kitchen. One twin scrapes food from each dinner plate into the garbage can and passes it to Francie, who dips it into the suds, letting her hands play among the hot bubbles. Her own face, when bubbles waft upward, is reflected in these rounded flying spheres. She sees her features in distorted permutations swirl through the air. Bubbles imprinted with her image land on the sweaters of the twins, clinging there an instant before vanishing.

She passes the dishes, one by one, to the right, into the other twin's long-fingered, powerful hand. He shakes off the excess water, wraps the plate in a flowered dishcloth, then dries it with awkward, irregular strokes.

So—this is the domestic life. It seems to have much to recommend it. The silent, repetitive actions lull Francie into a peaceful, trusting mood. She's warm, she's protected, she's enclosed, she's included. No words are necessary here; what could be said? And the twins seem, as always, to be in harmony, sharing the same thoughts or merely moving automatically in the vacuum of them.

Still, they are not totally unaware. Francie always feels the undercurrent of their attending to whatever it is Liz and Bill are doing. In this mode, the twins seem to be not birds, but a pair of hunting dogs whose ears are cocked in the direction of some invisible prey. They wait patiently, alertly, for the moment they will be called upon to act.

✴

The night is long. They are all becoming restless. Television does not hold their attention. Only so much reading, so much drafting can be done. If Francie and her friends still lived in the dorms, there might be a hall meeting, or a serenade out on the front porch, during which the "pinned" girl (the girl engaged-to-be-engaged to a fraternity boy) would be allowed outside wearing a prom gown, to stand alone as an entire fraternity appeared on the walkway, bearing candles, singing the song of their fraternity to honor her. If Bill and the twins still lived elsewhere, they'd be doing their nightly prowling, doing what men do, wandering about, drinking beers, driving out the Waldo Road to the all-night doughnut shop, possibly visiting at the homes of professors who enjoyed waxing wise into the wee hours.

But here: the six of them are doing what they can do here, limited by themselves and their present arrangement.

Bill paces the halls of the house; they hear the leather heels of his shoes echoing on the wooden floors. When he arrives back in the living room for the third time, he says why don't they borrow a car from the Grease Monkey garage and go joy-riding? There's a black Jaguar in the shop; it needs a good fast run on the highway, anyway. Why not? Nothing can happen to the car that he can't fix. How about it?

Bill, latching his fingers in his belt, standing with his legs spread like a cowboy on *Gunsmoke,* tells the doubting twins of the reason the car needs a high-speed test — something required for the carburetor. He dares them. Why not? Aren't they up to it? Francie remembers that kind of urchin dare from the faces of her boy cousins.

"Why not?" Liz echoes. "I'm getting restless. Let's do something. Let's go, let's just get out of here for some air."

Galvanized to action, the men get busy — they leave in the old Ford for the garage and are back in fifteen minutes with the Jag. Francie, Liz, and Amanda have, in the meantime, changed into dungarees and sweaters. They men toss some blankets into the trunk, pile in some firewood from the stack behind the French professor's house.

Someone directs Francie into the car so that she's in the back between the twins, while Liz is in the middle in the front, with Bill driving, Amanda at the window. The twins demonstrate how Francie should feel how soft the leather seats are, how supple to the touch. They both examine her face for reaction as she slides her hand over the upholstery. She exclaims duly. But to her a car is a car. It drives along. It has wheels and doors and headlights and something to steer with. It exists to take her out into the world, and in the world she is able to feel the wind on her face, to see the scenery shooting by. In the world she can watch the trees display their hanging masses of moss, which in the wind gives the illusion of old men and women whipping about their unkempt hair.

Bill and the twins call back and forth over the sound of air rushing in the windows, praising the smooth hum of the motor, the meshing of the gears, the absorption of the shocks. Amanda has let her golden hair fall over the back of the front seat. Her head keeps changing angles as if she is following with her eyes the path of the moon through the window.

Francie breathes deeply, tries to let go of all her cautions. She reminds herself that she could still be living in the dorms, signing in, signing out, listening to the chants of drunken men who want to own her panties as trophies. Instead, she tells herself, she is between two beautiful men in a Jaguar, she is speeding through the Gainesville night on a narrow country highway, she can smell the pine trees and the flowers and skunks and the essence of tarry road. She is alive, she is young, she is ready for adventure.

✗

At the Devil's Millhopper, Bill steers the Jaguar down the steep rocky road, bumping along in sharp, ominous jolts till the car comes to rest at the bottom of the sinkhole. They all sit in relief and silence for a few seconds, the men breathing deeply as if surprised at the ordeal of getting down here (and perhaps at the risk to the car).

Then they get busy pulling the blankets out of the trunk, unloading the firewood, stacking it in the center of the circular, barren clearing. In the headlights' beams, Francie sees there is nothing here but stone, hard jagged surfaces, emptiness.

The twins, engineers that they are, seem to be engineering something with Bill that goes on for too long. They huddle in the wind, whispering words that blow out of their mouths and disappear up the encircling stony walls and into the black night. Whistling across the top of the chasm is a truly frigid wind; the girls turn their backs to it, dancing about to keep warm. Finally the men get busy lighting the fire. When it flares, finally, jets of light smack strange images against the jagged walls of rock.

Francie feels an ebbing of her composure, her sense of adventure. She is almost certain she hears the sound of an approaching train, the roar getting louder and closer till she can feel the vibrations almost on top of her. Now she panics, convinced the train will plummet over the edge of the sinkhole and crush them all. She experiences one wild, brief regret for all the decisions that have led her to this time and place. She wants to pray for salvation—and the image to whom she realizes she wants to pray is the solid benevolent figure of Mary Ella Root.

*

Bill produces a bottle and offers it first to Liz. Liz takes a gulp and passes it to Francie. "Drink some, you'll get warm," Liz urges her, and she drinks, feeling a river of fire course down her throat, leaving dregs of bitterness on her tongue. "Now get down on the blanket," Liz instructs her. She obeys. She crouches. The wind isn't so fierce down below; she feels slightly warmer. She begins to relax, although the fire is blazing dangerously in the wind, whipping out red flares and pulling them back.

Matters are now out of her hands. She would like to give up control; she senses how deep a relief it would be to surrender her judgment, her powers of reasoning, her good sense. This, in itself, is a kind of logic—giving yourself up to those who know better, or know more, or tell you they do.

Bill and Liz seem to know what to do; they wrap themselves together, standing in the firelight, and cling tightly to each other, merging into one figure etched on the stone wall. The others look away, the twins standing uncertainly, rubbing their hands together, looking from Amanda, crouched on one blanket, to Francie, crouched on the other. The two men begin to pace like lions, their tall forms appearing in broken shards of shadow around the circular cage.

Some ceremony is about to take place, but what kind, and what for? Amanda, creeping about the blanket on her hands and knees, faces Francie and peers at her with these same questions in her face. What has never happened in the house is trying to happen here. Pairing is required. It is the law of the jungle. There is no civilization here, no speech, nothing but cold and the need to be close, be warm.

Suddenly Francie crawls toward Amanda, and Amanda, at the same time, begins to approach Francie on all fours. The two girls meet, throwing their arms about one another and laughing crazily. The twins, seeing this, fall to their knees on two corners of the two blankets and balance there, like odd, half-legged creatures, rocking on their kneecaps.

Whatever it is that is supposed to happen here, it seems, cannot. They are simply too cold, shivering violently, their teeth chattering like the ticking of unsynchronized clocks.

"Let's get the hell out of here," Bill growls. "This is the Arctic Circle."

"Or one of Dante's circles of hell," Liz says.

Relieved, clear now about how to take action, they whip the blankets back into the trunk, leave the fire to burn itself out in the rocky wasteland. Back in the car, trembling between the twins, Francie feels under her hand the leather seat, smooth as flesh, warm as life. She strokes it as if it were an animal, her pet.

As they drive back to the city, the twins doze, their heads lolling loosely from side to side till the head of one comes down to rest on Francie's right shoulder, and finally, the head of the other comes to rest on her left. She remains upright, alert, her eyes staring wide and excited into the dark, her gaze following the straight white line on the black road as it glows, moving into the mysterious future, illuminated only as far as the headlights are able to cast their brief, intense light.

# 12

# By Firelight

nable to sleep, Francie sits in the dark
kitchen at 3 A.M., staring out the window into the eye of a descending full
moon. The strangers who live in this
house with her are asleep, or so she imagines. This
night has been endless. The effects of the icy blasts of
sinkhole wind, having chilled them all to the bone,
could not easily be dispelled by the hot chocolate
Amanda prepared when they got back, or even by the
wood fire Bill started in the blackened brick fireplace.

Shivering, they sat in the living room for a long
while after they returned, each unwilling, it seemed, to
leave the company of the others. When one of the twins
complained about a spasm in his back, Liz offered to
massage the spot. The twin, whichever one he was,
readily crept onto the rug in front of the fireplace and
flattened himself, face down, like a hinged monkey.

Pulling up her sleeves in a businesslike way, Liz knelt and lifted the bottom of the twin's shirt, her face impassive. Francie tried to read Bill's expression as he sat on the couch in the dimness but was unable to understand how he might view this act. He simply sat, eyes unfocused, staring at the floor. Liz, in profile against the fire, moved her arms and hands efficiently over the bared muscles of the twin. Her beauty and boldness were amazing to Francie. As she labored over the twin, the contours of his back were illuminated by the flames, his muscles rippling under the force of Liz's thumbs. He lay limp, his head now turned to the side, his elbows jutting out in sharp triangles.

What, actually, was happening on that floor? Who belonged to whom here? *She* should have one of the twins for herself; why not? But what was allowed, what forbidden? She really knew none of them. They were strangers.

✳

At this moment, sitting at the table, Francie feels herself divided in two, like those black and white cookies of her childhood, each a flat entity with an iced surface of half chocolate, half vanilla. The surface tension that holds together the basic structure is barely substantial, the facade a dangerous, delicate glaze, easily cracked, easily melted. She isn't holding together, not safely— her state of being is one long vibration of desire, one long cry of need, puzzlement, and jealousy.

There's something else that worries her: the penis in her bedroom. It sits there incriminating as a murder weapon, handmade by her own hands. Last week, Liz had asked her if she wanted five pounds of clay left over from her art education class. In an idle hour when no one was in the house, Francie sat down at her desk and fashioned from it a thick and craggy male genital—so far as she could imitate one with verisimilitude—with a strange, curved erection. Her creation lacked detail, since Francie had never seen an adult model close up; she had a feeling, however, that it was probably. conceptually at least, correct.

The question was, why had she risked designing such a work of art? And now that she had, how was she to hide it? She thought she might make a miniature Japanese garden arrangement in which the arched gray penis could serve as a bridge over a lily pond. She could possibly even decorate it with folding toothpick-umbrellas, of the sort that came in club sandwiches in the Woolworth's downtown. Or dress the penis in a sock and lay it at the bottom of her drawer. Or simply squash it back into a lump of clay.

But no, she does not want to destroy it. She needs it. What she intends to do with it is not clear. It's a backup. It's a challenge. It's a private, dangerous secret.

✳

As she sits in the dark, there is a swishing of air in the hall; a twin passes by the kitchen on his way to the bathroom. Confident, no doubt, that his passage is un-observed, he glides past on bare feet, free as a panther in the dark. Francie makes herself invisible, holds her breath, hears him making water in the toilet, loud and forcefully, as clearly as if she stood beside him.

Francie lays her head on the tabletop and waits as the twin moves back through the hall to his room. *She is so lonely.* She presses her clenched fists into her cheeks and vows she will not be alone any longer. This certainty is upon her like a fever. Mary Ella tried to teach her this all along, but she was stubborn, stupid, resistant. Now the truth is totally clear: she is nothing without a man—every love poem, every play, every movie, every song, every single thought, message, work of art tells her so. Alone, she is as barren as the cold surface of the moon. Alone, she is almost dead.

✳

On the way to campus the next day, she plans that she will capture the first male she sees on the path. She will lasso a man; she will block his way and seduce him on a wooden bench. She considers some of the men in her classes: in French class there's Franco Lado, who is Spanish, who has a wonderful, long-legged way of walking. In her history class, there's the beautiful blue-eyed Frenchman, Emil, whose long, graceful fingers caress his pen as he takes notes. A boy named Franz who works in the student union always flirts with her at lunch time when she pushes her tray along the silver bars. She senses an open-heartedness in foreign men that makes them more approachable. Unlike American boys, they seem to value something in women more meaningful than the usual beauty-queen, big-bosomed essence of female. They tend to look for the beauty within, where—Francie's sure, if she has any—hers is.

If she has any.

# 13

## *Tosca*

An overdue paper, the first late assignment in Francie's school career, is inching out of her typewriter slow as hot tar. She's been writing for two days but has been reluctant (and ashamed) to reveal her true interpretation of Tolstoy's grief-ridden *Anna Karenina*. Frankly, she thinks Anna made a perfectly sensible choice by throwing herself under the train. She's worried, however, that if she turns in her paper with this conclusion, she may find herself picked up by attendants in white and be hurried off to the school psychiatrist. Who knows if Dr. Raskolnikov is duty-bound by university rules to report any student who seems to take a positive view of suicide?

Anna Karenina, who, by the time she decides to end it all, has experienced more of life than Francie can ever hope to know. Anna, a woman of high station and great beauty, has—besides having had two men who love her desperately—known thrilling romance, sexual passion, the pangs of childbirth, the fulfillments of mother-love, and, in truth, every emotion that makes life worthwhile.

Francie reasons that if Anna wants to throw herself under a train, that's her business. If—on the other hand—Francie should decide to end it all now, she'd have missed almost all of it! No one has danced with her in great ballrooms, no one has adored her body and soul, and not a single man has followed her to the ends of the earth with a wild hunger to be in her presence.

Writing this paper for Dr. Raskolnikov has been a torture. Francie knows she can hardly express her true opinion of Anna's actions and still appear sane. Her struggles between term paper protocol and her own radical convictions are what have delayed her finishing this paper and prevented her from turning it in, yesterday, Friday afternoon, when it was due.

Now she is on her wobbly last page, summing up her convictions (finally!) about the uselessness of existence if one lives to old age without experiencing the grand passions of life.

There's nothing more she can do with it. She's done. She's spoken her mind and now will have to take her chances on getting a passing grade or getting herself referred to a mental health specialist. Her one hope is to stand on the grounds that *Anna Karenina,* in the final analysis, has all the requirements that Dr. Raskolnikov offered to their class as the requirement for great literature. Without a doubt it has:

Friction
Love
Unfaithfulness
Forgiveness
Forever After.

Unfortunately, in Anna's case, the notion of "Forever After" is equivalent not to happy-forever-after but to dead-forever-after. Even so, it does sum things up and end the story in a satisfactory manner.

Francie types "The End," rolls out the paper, and fastens all the sheets together with a silver paper clip. She sits back at her desk in the creaky rocking chair and sighs. The Gainesville afternoon is dark and chill; the bare leaves of a tree are scraping in the wind against her window. The big house is silent; her housemates are either studying, sleeping, or not home. She has not encountered a single one of them today. If Liz and Amanda have finished their papers for this class, they have not discussed their efforts with Francie. She finds it harder—not easier—to talk with them about anything these days.

She double checks in the phone book for the address of Dr. Raskolnikov. His house is only three blocks from here; she plans to deliver her paper directly into his hands, rather than wait till Monday to bring it to his office.

Tying the belt of her aqua wool coat tightly around her waist, she walks along the quiet street, kicking leaves with the white toes of her saddle shoes. It is Saturday, late afternoon: the time when girls in the sorority houses and dorms are doubtless setting their hair and painting their nails for the evening's parties, dates, and festivities. The fraternity boys are certain to be plotting their schemes and seductions, getting in their supplies of beer, arranging to borrow cars or use the apartments of friends who live off campus.

A few tears well up in Francie's eyes. Self-pity, that disgusting, delicious indulgence (she thinks), is the one deserved privilege of all lonely girls. Like Anna K., she could head for the train station, wait till the milk train from Ocala came shooting by, and dive under its wheels. She smiles bitterly, imagining the commotion it would cause; her bloody coat, the pages of her term paper blown along the tracks, Liz and Amanda white with shock when they got the news, the twins stopped dead in their mechanical tin-soldier movements long enough to realize they hadn't been very kind to her. Even Bill might think about how he had mostly ignored his kinship with her, their missed opportunity, the secret bond of their shared history.

Well, her mangled body wouldn't deter any of them from their pleasures for long. It hardly paid to waste a thought considering them. In no time at all they'd be back watching *Gunsmoke* and eating ice cream.

But what of her parents? When Francie imagines

their horror and grief at her demise, she rejects the whole idea permanently.

✳

As it turns out, Professor Raskolnikov is in front of his house sweeping up leaves into a great triangular pile with a straw broom. He's wearing floppy blue-and-white striped pants and a sweatshirt with a huge yellow parrot on it. Perched on his head is a red knit stocking cap with a white tassel at the end.

Francie calls to him politely. He jumps, clearly startled, and pulls his stocking cap from his head. He thrusts the broom between his legs and tops it with the hat while he smoothes his wavy hair back with both hands.

"Well!" he says. "What are you doing in these parts, young lady?"

Francie indicates the folder in her hand. "I didn't want to turn this in later than I had to," she explains, "though I am sorry, it is a little late."

"You needn't have worried," Professor R. says generously. "Not you, one of my best students." He looks toward his wooden house, and then toward Francie, who turns in the direction of his glance. She sees a person she can't place at first, a young man who appears in the doorway of the house. Then she realizes it is the young Frenchman from her history class, Emil. He is holding in his hands a steaming coffee cup.

"Aha," he calls." Francie! How nice to see you! Do you and Leon know one another?"

"Well, if this is Leon, then he's my Russian lit professor," Francie says.

"How very interesting," Emil says in his heart-stopping French accent. Emil's face is fair, his cheeks shade to a delicate pink. He is simply a blue-eyed blond, a combination extremely common, but its aesthetic perfection never fails to affect Francie.

Emil continues to stand in the doorway. Professor R. swings on his broomstick.

"Do you live here?" Francie says to Emil. She doesn't know what made her say it—she just did.

The two men look at one another.

"Look," Professor R. says. "Why don't you come in and have some coffee, won't you?"

✳

The living room of the small house smells fragrant: Francie identifies incense and the fading leaves of dying fresh flowers. The ashy odor of scorched logs rises from the fireplace. From across the room, an aria sung by a soprano shimmers into the air as a record turns on the phonograph. Francie looks around, wondering if she should have declined to come in, seeing the soft dented cushions on the couch, other pillows tossed on the floor. A dish of salted peanuts sits on the coffee table. She remembers what Liz and Amanda said about her teacher. Is it true, then, that he is one of those men who love men? If she can love men, why couldn't anyone be susceptible to loving men? And, along that same line of thinking, couldn't she be a woman who loves women?

She thinks of Liz's beauty, the shape of her arms, the delicacy of her wrists; she pictures the light on Amanda's cheekbones, the slight trill of her laughter. But no—though she can admire and wish to be like other women, it is definitely a man she wants. Never mind what she has been told: that a man is the cover to her pot, her better half, the yin to her yang, her rescuer, her Prince Charming, all that she needs to be complete. Though she discounts these bits of homey wisdom as nonsense, she knows her truth to be not fairy tale but visceral necessity.

Emil, his hair a tangle of blonde curls, offers Francie a cup of coffee. She doesn't know whether to accept or not, to sit down or to leave. She takes the cup from his fingers and nearly drops it. "Oh—this is hot," she says and sets it on the table.

"How do you like that angel, Maria Callas?" he says, cocking his ear to the music. An endless, impossibly pure high note is hanging in the air. "Listen to that—when she suffers, I bleed. When she soars to the heavens, I myself am flying." Emil folds himself to the floor and lays back on a pile of cushions. When he stares heavenward, Francie follows his gaze. To her astonishment, she sees that the ceiling of the room is covered with record jackets, dozens of them, taped to the plaster. She reads the titles of famous operas: *Tosca, The Magic Flute, Aida, Carmen, Faust, Rigoletto, La Bohème*.

"She dies at the end, of course," Professor R. says.

"Of course," echoes Emil.

"Well, Anna Karenina dies at the end," Francie ventures. "In my paper. In the novel, I mean. A novel is not an opera, of course," she adds.

"But it is like one. All great love stories are like operas," Professor R. says.

"And so many great love stories end in death . . . or parting, which is like death," says Emil.

"Not all," Professor R. replies. "Sometimes there is an exception."

"But most love stories do end badly," Emil insists.

Francie feels she is out of her depth here. "You may not agree with my paper," Francie says cautiously, "but I took a chance and wrote that I think Anna Karenina lived a full life. She had the great love of her life before she died. So maybe Tolstoy is saying she had all there is to have."

"You may be on the right track."

"As was Anna," Emil says, and laughs. "Right on the track."

"Funny, my friend," says Francie's professor. The men look at one another and their eyes hold for a moment.

Francie takes a sip of coffee, still hot enough to burn her tongue. "I should be going," she says. "But thank you very much for inviting me in." She sets her cup down and makes her way toward the door, stepping among the pillows on the floor.

"Come again," Emil says. "And I shall look for you in history class."

"Yes," Francie says. "See you there."

Once she is outside, she realizes she has been half-holding her breath. She feels faint. On her way home, she eliminates Emil from the list of men she might hope to conquer.

Oh, this business of love. What *is* love? How does one find it?

It is the aria she sings to herself under the darkening winter sky.

# 14

# Every Pot Has a Cover

The penis can be reshaped to any form once the clay is warmed in Francie's hands. She can divide it in three and braid it into a *challah*. She can make it into a circle, a square, a diamond. She can form it into a bunny, a kitten, a snake. What she decides to do today is make, from the remainder of the clay still kept moist in a plastic bag, two balls. She feels this an act of anarchy, dangerous, on the edge. At any moment, someone could knock at the door of her room, ask to come in. Someone could find her attaching two balls to the base of the penis. She could be caught in the act.

Oh, what a brave girl! Such a dangerous act, playing with clay. Such risk, that someone might actually knock at her door. The fact is, no one is home. The twins and Bill are at the garage, Liz and Amanda at the library. And the truly forbidden act, what Liz and Bill must actually do in one or the other one of their rooms, is not done with clay, is not playing. The two of them are no longer mere housemates; they are mates. The way they look at each other, go off together, leaving the rest of them dumbstruck and sitting awkwardly in the living room, is proof. In fact, this living together as a family, this brave experiment, seems to have fallen flat altogether.

For some reason, cooking at home in their own kitchen has failed as one of the great attractions of living off campus. The twins have a taste that runs to black-eyed peas, grits, biscuits, and ham. These are foods not simple to prepare at the house and much easier to have dished onto a plate at the student union or the College Inn on University Avenue. Liz and Amanda have a preference for salads and green vegetables, and Bill makes it a point to drive up to a delicatessen in Jacksonville every week to bring back a stock of kosher hot dogs, sour pickles, corned beef, knishes, and bagels. The novelty of a shared domestic life among the six of them is beginning to wear thin. Lately, for her own meals, Francie has begun buying Wonder Bread and jars of peanut butter and apple jelly at the Piggly Wiggly. The six of them have given up the pretense that they all eat together, or even that they live together. They wander into the kitchen separately, or sometimes two at a time, or just go out as they please, with no explanations to anyone else.

Now and then Francie actually feels nostalgic about

Mary Ella Root; she misses her old roommate, that simple, good-hearted soul who was always happy to discuss bridal fashions and the odds of marrying before graduation. Francie wonders if she is still praying for a date, or praying merely for her Face-Lifter to do its work.

In fact, Francie thinks frequently about the girls in her old dormitory, all of them trying to stay virgins and not all of them succeeding. Some girls were inclined—almost by nature—to be "good," while others had a vital need to be "bad." Even Francie's literary heroines come as one of the two types. Edna St. Vincent Millay burned her candle at both ends; Katherine Anne Porter took off to live in Mexico after the Revolution; the French writers, like Colette, like Françoise Sagan (whom Francie has just read this summer) danced casually in and out of their lovers' beds. On the other side were Virginia Woolf, who wore long woolen sweaters and found sex highly overrated, and Emily Dickinson, who lived indoors, cloistered, flitting—ghostly in white—from room to room.

None of them, it had to be admitted, were of Jewish stock, which might be why Francie can't truly identify with any of them. No doubt the mothers of the writers she admires weren't constantly dispensing warnings of the sort dealt Francie by her Jewish mother and aunts. Where can she find a Jewish role model who celebrates the sensual life? Thomas Wolfe, she knows, had a Jewish mistress, but Francie does not think she and Aline Bernstein are kindred spirits.

✳

The clay is soft enough to work on, and Francie decides she has to give the sculpted penis some texture. She knows that Liz still has some carving tools she keeps in a small wooden box in her room; she will just go in there and try to find the scraper and shaper she needs. Francie closes the door to her room and goes down the hall. Though no one is home, though no one is supposed to be home, she knocks on Liz's door for safety, then enters. She sees the box at once, on top of the old dresser. Instead of taking it and leaving, she finds herself opening the top drawer of Liz's dresser. Her hands seem to know what she wants to do before she knows it herself.

And there it is. Proof! The long, thin box of contraceptive jelly. Inside (Francie carefully opens the cardboard container) is the tube, rolled up at the bottom. And at the side of the box is the clear plastic inserter, not entirely clear, but blurred with a residue of jelly. So of course they are doing it. The forbidden act. Isn't Liz worried about becoming pregnant? About not being a good girl? About being ruined?

Francie goes back to her room. She leaves the sculpting tools behind. She is now repelled by the idea of touching the cold clay penis. Never mind texture. Never mind balls. She drops the penis down to the bottom of her dirty laundry bag, grabs her books, and leaves the house. She has to go somewhere, somewhere she's welcome. Or, at least, where she's not unwelcome.

"You want to have a beer?"

"What?"

Francie is standing at the check-out desk in the library when Harvey Rubin comes up behind her and speaks so close to her ear she feels his breath. She's known him since high school. He's a transplant from New York, as she is. His parents run a restaurant in Miami Beach. Harvey is majoring in psychology and likes to test his theories of human behavior on Francie. One of them is about surprise attack, like this one.

"I don't like beer."

"Come anyway."

"I need to study."

"You can study human behavior while we have a beer."

"Okay."

Harvey points out how easily she has caved in as they walk up University Ave. "Francie, any guy could talk you into bed. Look how fast you agreed to come with me."

"You're not any guy, Harvey. And you're not trying to get me into bed."

"How do you know?" Harvey says. He rolls his eyes at her, like Groucho Marx. He looks a little like him, too, with his thick dark hair, substantial nose, and antic expression.

"Don't get started," Francie says. "I'm in a bad mood."

"Tell Papa Freud about it."

"I wouldn't know where to start."

"You tell me your love problems, I'll tell you mine." He holds open the door of the student hangout next to the College Inn. They slide into a dim booth toward the back. There's a flashing neon beer sign on the wall just above their booth. Francie watches it gratefully. She is just so relieved to be somewhere other than in her room.

"You wish you had some love problems," Francie says.

"But I do. Did I tell you, I'm in love with Patty Bluehart? She plays oboe," Harvey says. "I hang around in the Music Building, I stand right outside her practice room. Sometimes I peek into the little window in the door. Yesterday I saw her wetting a reed with her mouth—you know how oboe players roll the reeds around with their tongues? I thought I would faint, watching her do things with her tongue and lips."

"I'm not really familiar with that practice," Francie says. She stops talking as the waitress comes by and takes their order.

"Francie, seriously, why do you think women don't like me?"

"Oh, stop it, Harvey," she says. "One day some woman will."

"How do you know?"

"Because everyone knows, there's a pot for every

cover. Or a cover for every pot, I forget which. I've heard it since the day I was born."

"Your mother told you that?"

"Well, she said she couldn't promise me exactly when it would happen or who it would be, but she could guarantee it would definitely happen sometime because that was the way the world worked."

"What kind of crazy way is that to think?"

"The Jewish way," Francie says.

The waitress comes back and sets two beers down on the table.

"And the cover for her pot . . . is she happy with it?" Harvey asks.

"You mean my father? Who knows?" Francie says. "They're married. They got what they wanted. Now they don't have to think about it anymore."

"I think about it all the time," Harvey says. "I think about women so much I levitate off my bed. I don't study. I might even flunk out of school."

"Then you'll be drafted," she warns. "Bill worries about that—he got a warning letter. His grades are pretty bad."

Harvey knows all about her living situation; he likes to present his theories to her about the dynamics of their "ménage à six."

"So tell me," he asks now, "if Bill gets drafted, will the twins run off with Liz and share her happily ever after?"

"Not likely. It's more likely Liz will run off with Bill.

They're very . . . involved." She doesn't trust Harvey enough to tell him what she's just discovered.

"Involved, eh?" Harvey says. He takes a gulp of his beer. "Lucky guy. She's so beautiful."

Francie bends her head and sips the bitter drink. Her feelings are suddenly hurt; she knows Liz is beautiful. She knows she isn't. But Harvey didn't have to say that. She's suddenly annoyed with him and considers telling him why women don't like him. He's too needy. He announces everything that he thinks. What he doesn't have, and can't get, is written all over him. What women want is a man who is self-contained, confident, who can stand on his own. At least, Francie decides, that's the kind of man she would like.

She sits silently for a while, trying to drink her beer, wondering why anyone could like something that tastes this bad. A chocolate ice cream soda is what she'd really like now, with lots of whipped cream.

"I ought to get back to the library," she tells Harvey.

"Let's go over to the Music Building first," he says. "To see if Patty might be practicing her oboe." When she hesitates, Harvey adds, "Maybe you'll meet the man of your dreams. There's some guy who looks like Tony Curtis who's always practicing over there. Sensitive fingers and so on."

"Okay," she agrees. "Why not? I'm in no hurry. Let's go."

# 15

# Music of the Spheres

Winds of dissonance, sounding to Francie like shrieks and moans from the underworld, shudder through the hollow wooden halls of the Music Building. She hangs back at the entrance because of the din.

"Come on," Harvey Rubin insists—"into the breach."

But she's frozen on the threshold, trying to separate the voices of flutes, clarinets, tubas, drums, the dueling of pianos, the clattering racket of metronomes and marimbas. From an upper floor, she hears what sounds like a choir of mad singers, each one holding a note longer, higher, lower, deeper, wilder than the others.

"Come on." Harvey takes her hand and pulls her along.

"How do they stand the racket?" Francie asks. "How do they hear themselves?"

Harvey is now stopping to peer into the glass window of one small room, then another. He pushes Francie in front of him so that she can see inside. The back of each musician is toward the window—a violinist bends toward the music on the stand before her, a cellist sits on a folding chair, her legs spread wide, holding the instrument that resembles another female form against her knees.

Francie draws away, sensing she is intruding on each musician's private communion, her deepest intimacy. A wave of heat is running up her back and face; her heart is pounding.

Harvey looks at her, says knowingly, "It's exciting, isn't it? When I first saw Patty Bluehart with her oboe, wetting the mouthpiece, the way her tongue was focused on that mouthpiece, I went to pieces. I don't know if she's here today . . . or the Tony Curtis look-alike I told you about. Let's keep looking."

Francie pauses to drink from the water cooler. When she lifts her face, water dripping from her mouth, Harvey is motioning her over to the door of a room.

"In there," he whispers. "Hurry."

Francie presses her face to the glass and sees a dark-haired young man in a short-sleeved shirt. His head is bent forward over the keys; his arms are powerful, manly, covered with dark, curly hair. The muscles of his back ripple as he plays; his concentration seems extreme. Her eye is drawn to the fingers of his right hand as they play a trill. She almost feels the vibration, like a chill, going down her back.

The man seems to sense someone at the door and suddenly turns around. She steps back to hurry after Harvey, who is just turning the corner, disappearing from her sight.

The practice room door opens. "Wait!" The young man is far more beautiful than Tony Curtis, though there is a resemblance, the way his dark hair curls over his forehead, the sensual curve of his mouth. "Sorry." He's addressing Francie. "I've gone over my time. It's hard to get a slot to practice; these rooms are always booked up. You must be waiting to play."

"Oh, no," Francie says. "I'm not a musician. I just heard you playing. I wanted to see who could play so beautifully. You must be very talented."

"Talent is plentiful," he says. "It's all over the place. Real genius is what's rare."

"I'm sure," Francie says. "But wouldn't it be nice to be a genius? I'm not one, either."

"Well, we're a pair, then," the young man says.

She looks up at his face to see if he means to be clever, if he's going to follow up, introduce himself, ask her name. But he's already stepped back into the room, his back to her; he's begun turning pages of the music book on the piano, finding the next piece he wants to practice. He sits down, adjusts the bench, folds the page back so it doesn't close itself, and begins to play.

He's forgotten Francie. She quietly closes the door and turns down the hall to find the water fountain again. She's burning, desperately thirsty. The spurting water runs down her chin, into the V of the neckline of her blouse. To collect herself, she reads a few announcements on a bulletin board, then goes outside to sit on the steps. Eventually Harvey comes out of the Music Building to report that Patty Bluehart and her oboe are nowhere to be seen.

"My heart is broken."

"You'll live," Francie says.

✳

On Saturday morning, at the house, something is in the air. Conspiracy is what Francie senses, whispers that stop when she appears, glances that don't meet her eye. The twins are at the kitchen table working on their drawings or equations or whatever it is that they do, but they both seem stalled, not really working. Both of them are doodling on the edges of their notebook paper. Amanda is walking about rather aimlessly, her hair in rollers, studying an eyelash curler she holds before her. It's a metal device that traps eyelashes between two edges of a rubber clamp and bends them upward. Francie is familiar with its workings because Mary Ella Root used one often.

"Do you need help with that?" Francie asks.

"Oh, no, thank you!" Amanda says. "I don't think I'll actually use it. I think I might blind myself."

Liz, breathless, is dancing from room to room, her pale fair skin flushed with heat.

"Is something going on?" Francie says to her, standing in the open door of the bathroom while Liz takes down from the shower rack her hand-washed and now dry underwear.

"Well, I guess I have to tell you. I was trying to think of how to break this to you, Francie, but I didn't want to hurt your feelings."

"What?" Francie imagines that they are going to ask her to leave the house, that she will be out in the street, homeless. "What is it!"

"I'm getting married, Francie."

*"What?"*

"Bill and I are getting married. Tonight. In Jacksonville. We're all leaving here in a few minutes. But the problem is, I'm not inviting you to the wedding."

"I really don't understand," Francie says, leaning against the doorframe of the bathroom. She notes, foolishly, that the showerhead is dripping water, drop by drop.

"Come into my room," Liz says, and Francie follows her down the hall. On Liz's bed is an open suitcase, half-packed.

"The thing is," Liz continues, "that Amanda is going to be my maid of honor and the twins are going to be Bill's best men, and the truth is, we're borrowing a car from the garage that isn't big enough for all of us, so please don't be angry if you can't be at my wedding, Francie."

"I can't be at your wedding? Why is there a wedding now? Are you pregnant?"

"Don't be silly, Francie. I'm too smart for that. But Bill's grades have really fallen this year, and his draft board's just notified him that his student deferment is over, that he's definitely going to be drafted. So Bill decided he's going to beat them and join up first. If the Russians decide to blast us with missiles, he'll be right there to send an atom bomb right back. He's sick of school and says he'd rather fight than study, anyway. So the twins will run the garage while he's gone. Bill's leaving next week for basic training. That's why we decided we have to get married right now. To make everything clear to both of us. To make it legal. To make *us* legal."

Francie looks around the room—a vision of the contraceptive jelly comes into her mind. Then she thinks of being left alone here all weekend . . . just her and her clay penis.

Liz must see something on Francie's face that makes her come over and give Francie a hug. "It's really nothing personal, Francie, there's just no room in the car. That's all. This is no big affair, we're going to a justice of the peace tonight, and then Amanda and the twins are taking the train back to Gainesville and Bill and I are going to spend the weekend—our honeymoon—in

Jacksonville. Then on Monday we'll be back, and on Friday Bill will ship out, and everything will be the same here . . . except that Bill won't be here anymore. He'll be serving Uncle Sam."

"But Bill *hates* Uncle Sam," Francie says. It's all she can think of to say.

"Well, that may be true, but he likes to be in control. So this is his way of doing it. On his own terms."

"Well," Francie says, "Then congratulations, I guess."

"You're not mad?" Liz asks. "Please don't be."

"I just didn't think you had the slightest interest in rushing off to get married before graduation. You seemed so . . . hostile to that idea."

"Well, here I am," Liz says, twirling around for Francie's benefit. "The blushing bride."

✳

Once the wedding party has driven off, once Francie realizes that she is alone in the house, she feels a stirring of panic. This marriage business is dead serious; every female on campus is imprinted with this need, even Liz, the iconoclast. Yet, Francie herself is light years away from marriage. How does one achieve it? How does one simply pick a man and decide to live the rest of life with him? Furthermore—and this is perhaps the crudest part of love—a woman picks a mate because he *is* a man; that's her very first and primal consideration. She looks to see if he shaves and has the right private parts and only then considers if this is one she could bear to marry.

Francie really can't stand thinking about this another minute. She must get out of here. Where can she go? She doesn't want to stay here alone and think. She'll go . . . to see the alligator. She'll go . . . to the movies downtown. She'll go . . . and have a beer. Maybe she'll cut off her hair, yes, cut it very short. Or maybe she'll join a sorority. Or go into town and buy more clay. She'll fill the house with penises of varying sizes—that should entertain the newlyweds when they get back!

She is not really sane. So she gets her purse and decides to go to Broward Hall to visit Mary Ella Root.

✻

In the lobby of her old dorm, Francie breathes deeply, feeling she's returned to a place of her youth, to a time long outgrown. Girls are everywhere—at the desk, at the mail boxes, waiting on line to fill in their sign-out cards. From the lounge she hears the piano being played and glances in to see what's going on. As usual, girls are there, too, watching some guy playing the piano. In fact, six girls are draped along the edges of it. She listens to hear whether the song being played is "Heart and Soul" or a variation of "Chopsticks." But no—today it's the real thing. A Bach invention spills forth from the piano, all clarity and sharp brightness. Then Francie stops short, feeling her heart shake. She recognizes that the piano player is the young man from the Music Building. Far from "Chopsticks," far from "Heart and Soul," or "The Tennessee Waltz," he is playing music of another realm. The half dozen girls are ooh-ing and aah-ing, leaning here and there, arranging their hips against the polished mahogany sides of the piano and leaning their breasts on the lid. Francie hesitates, watches for a moment, but she certainly won't join them, add her adoring expression and cashmere sweater set and circle skirt to the mix (though she, too, is wearing just such a sweater set and skirt).

One girl asks him if he knows "Hold Me, Thrill Me, Kiss Me."

He doesn't even look up.

Francie leaves the lounge and goes up the ramp to her old wing. She hurries along the hall toward the room she used to share with Mary Ella Root. At the public phone on the wall, she can see the hanging clipboard with the usual messages: BCNM: Boy Called, No Message, or BCWCB: Boy Called, Will Call Back.

The door to her old room is ajar, and she peeks in. There's Mary Ella, rooted to her bed as if she has not got off once since Francie moved away.

"Hello, Mary Ella."

"Oh, my God! Is it Francie? Bless my soul! You shocked me, nearly sent me to my maker. Honeybun, what on earth are you doing here? Do you want to come back and live here with me again? Or—oh, my God—did you come to tell me some news?"

"News?" Francie asks. She glances at the neatly made second bed that was once hers. She doesn't even know the name of Mary Ella's new roommate. She feels sad, as if she's moved far away to a life that doesn't suit her as well as the safe, old one.

"I mean, you know . . . boyfriend-news, husband-news. Graduation is just around the corner; this is our last gasp, sweetheart. I thought maybe, at least by now, you were pinned."

"Nothing like that, Mary Ella. But you remember Liz? She's getting married! Tonight, in fact! Isn't that a surprise! Only I'm just the same as before. But who knows, as you always say, maybe a miracle will happen."

Mary Ella smiles coyly. "Miracles do happen." She wiggles her hand at Francie, who at first does not understand what she is meant to see. Then it dawns on her: Mary Ella is wearing an engagement ring.

"Oh, Mary Ella! Who is he? When did it happen?" The breath has gone out of her; she is truly shocked. This is too much for one day.

"Come see his picture," she says with reverence and lifts a gold and glass frame from her desk, holding it toward Francie. "Freddy Watkins," she says proudly. "Six foot five."

What Francie sees is a flat-faced, rosy-skinned, overweight, crew-cut boy with a big, warm smile.

"How did it happen so fast, Mary Ella? I mean, how . . . where?"

"Love strikes like a rattler, honey. First it's under a

rock, and then it strikes right in the center of your heart."

"Well, that's wonderful, Mary Ella. But where was he hiding, and how did he find you?"

Mary Ella begins to tell the story of how she lost her eyeglass case in the student union, and, since her name and address were in it, Freddy was kind enough to return it.

As Francie listens to this simple and ordinary story, she actually feels tears welling up in her eyes.

"Oh! Don't you despair, darling. You're ripe, you know. We're living right in the range of time all this is supposed to happen; it's nature's plan, it could happen to you even today. Or tomorrow. I never gave up, and don't you." To prove to Francie how certain she is that all is not lost, Mary Ella pulls her bulk off the bed and comes to hug her.

"I predict . . ." Mary Ella Root says, "and I have a special gift, you know—one of my grandmothers was a fortuneteller—I predict that before you graduate you will meet the man of your dreams."

"It better happen fast," Francie says. "I have only a couple of months—I really don't have a minute to waste." For that moment, she wants to lean her head against Mary Ella's breast, she wants to believe her, she wants someone else to figure it all out for her. She understands that Mary Ella is wise, has wisdom, after all. Francie never gave her credit for this, for having any sense at all . . . and now she envies her. Mary Ella has faith. She trusts in the future. Where does a person find a faith like that, Francie wonders.

✳

When Francie leaves, taking with her a copy of *Bride's* magazine that Mary Ella presses upon her for inspiration, she again hears piano music coming from the lounge. The young man with dark curly hair is still playing the piano, something atonal and harsh—the six girls have drifted away. In fact, no one but the young man at the piano is in the lounge at all.

Francie hesitates only briefly. Then she walks in and leans herself against the side of the piano. She waits out Bartok, an étude of Chopin, and then more Bach.

When he finally looks up, Francie smiles at him. "Hi," she says.

When recognition dawns in his eyes, she says, "There's really a very fine line that divides talent from genius," Francie says. "I wouldn't be too hard on yourself. Maybe you are a genius. Maybe you really are. You shouldn't judge yourself too fast."

# 16

# Letter Home (2)

Though Francie's mother writes her almost daily, her father never does. Her mother, who works as a secretary in a real estate office, types long, chatty letters from her office recounting what she made for dinner the night before, describing the dog's antics, the state of the weather, the landlord's refusal to fix the broken sink. Francie reads her letters impatiently, irritably, as if listening to a long, monotonal song. There will be nothing in her mother's news that she can apply to her life, and writing an answer is always an interruption in her reveries, which she goes to great pains to conceal.

But one day a letter arrives from her father:

*Hiya Francie,*
*I know that it's about time I wrote to you, sweetheart, though being a "lefty" means you probably won't even be*

able to make out my handwriting. All your letters are
looked forward to, and we are all happy that you are
happy. Are you getting any ideas for your journalism class?
I remember you did that piece you sent us: "The Treacher-
ous Tick: A Menace to Your Dog." I've just thought of an
Idea for Ideas—get old pop songs and put a few together
and I bet you'd have lots of material. It's just a thought—
might not be any good. I'm sorry I couldn't locate the desk
lamp sooner. Some day I'll fix it and send it off to you. I
bet you can use more of your record collection. Tell us
which ones you want and I'll ship them to you.

Did you figure out why I call Skippy "Ukulele"? "My
Dog Has Fleas." Ho-Ho. Well, I'm not ho-ho-ing so much
since next week I'm going to have some of my teeth removed and get partial dentures. Your Dad is getting to be
an old man. I just don't believe it. My knees tell me it's the
truth, though.

Sorry, Dear, my letter seems very flat to me, but it's
just gossip and hellos. Well, since I'm about written out
for this letter, I'll close with—

Be Good,
Be Kindly,
Be Generous,
Be Yourself,
Behave,
Be My Girl,
Be My Valentine,
Be Healthy,
Be Wise,

*Beware,*
*Be Wealthy, and, above all, Francie, light of my life,*
*Be Happy,*

                 *Love and Kisses from Your Dad.*

Reading this letter makes Francie cry because her father loves her and wants her to be happy and he knows that she is not. The letter makes her cry because she has not ever really been happy and now—she thinks—happiness may actually be within her reach. Her mother, who accepts unhappiness as a normal state of affairs, expects less from life than her father and never sends Francie such heartfelt, hopeful messages.

Still, against her better judgment, she is moved by a wild and urgent need to reassure them, to relieve them (especially her father) of any guilt for bringing her into this life. She knows how dangerous it is for her to confide in them, especially since what is happening to her is so very new, so very extreme and unclear, but she's driven to prove to them she—like any ordinary daughter—might find joy in life and might, in the words of her grandmother, bring them *naches*. So she sits down to type them a letter.

*Dear Mom and Dad:*

*I have some exciting news to tell you: I've finally met a nice Jewish boy, which I know has been your hope for me. His name is Joshua, and people say he looks like the actor Tony Curtis. Mom, you'll be happy to hear he's a pianist, like you. Thank heaven you made me take piano lessons when I was young. Though I wasn't good at it and never practiced, I want to assure you it hasn't all been a waste; at least when I talk to Joshua, I know the difference between major and minor keys and what a fugue is. Maybe some day, Mom, you and he can play duets together. He is taking me this weekend to the Classic Film Series to see* Beauty and the Beast—*in French. So I'm doing fine right now and feeling happy. And, Dad, I loved your last letter. Even if you don't have all real teeth, your smile will always be beautiful to me. Love from Francie.*

✳

That night Francie dreams: *I am under a tree with Joshua and his mother sticks a straight pin in my lip. Joshua cries out to her, "Don't blame her; we are going rowing together." We each drink tea out of a cup of stars, and the tea tastes like lilacs. When the branches of the tree rustle in the wind, tiny baby rattlesnakes with human faces drop down on us, sweetly, like confetti.*

✳

What it means, she can't guess. But it's rich and strange, connected to the thing that's happening, the thing with a man that has never happened to her before, the connection she feels is taking shape.

✳

Because time is now telescoped, because Francie can hardly distinguish night from day, morning from evening, she recognizes that her entire purpose in life is concentrated in one little rock of need: *Be with Joshua.* And it has happened to him, as well. He tells her he wants to be with her all the time. How could this have transformed their lives so fast? Neither of them questions it. The two of them somehow have agreed to bypass chatter, getting-to-know-you formalities, the bow-and-curtsey of dates, dinners, movies, ice-cream sodas. They seem to have moved from the piano bench to the bench under the tree without transition, a forceful glide into passion, into a turbulence and heat such as Francie has never known.

She's not herself. When Amanda and the twins come back from Jacksonville, she barely questions them about the wedding. When Liz and Bill return from their brief honeymoon, she gives them—for a present—a big, frozen, white cheesecake on a lace doily that she bought in the Piggly Wiggly. When, at the next weekend, Bill leaves for basic training at Fort Benning, Georgia, even when Liz closes herself in her room in tears, Francie can't respond to this. She has moved to another level of existence; she doesn't care what contraceptive aids Liz has in her dresser drawer or what the twins do in their beds or in the toilet, she no longer watches other couples kiss in doorways, she is barely aware of her own daily routines—class, library, term papers, tests. What she lives for is this:

Joshua comes to call for her at the house at dinner time. They walk down the pleasant neighborhood street, walk several long blocks, under trees laden with buds of spring blossoms, and then across the campus to the student union. When she looks sideways at him, at his strong face, the way he sometimes holds his chin tilted at an angle, at his lock of curly hair that falls over his forehead, he reminds her of a beautiful wild horse.

They enter the student union and leave their schoolbooks on a high shelf with the books of other students. They each select a tray and slide it (Francie goes first) over the silver rails to the place where steaming foods are displayed: hot dogs and beans, fried catfish and French fries, meatloaf and mashed potatoes, spaghetti and meatballs. They move on; each one chooses his desired food, a carton of milk, chooses (always, they both do) a slice of pecan pie, chooses silverware, napkins, an empty glass for the milk.

They walk (Joshua goes first) toward the back of the cafeteria till he finds an out-of-the-way table for them, a table in a corner, facing a blank wall, and they sit down, facing the blank wall so that no one is likely to greet them or come over to chat. They eat with hunger, quickly but pleasantly, looking at each other's face and smiling from time to time. Sometimes Joshua makes a comment, sometimes Francie, but mainly they are fortifying themselves for the long evening ahead.

The pecan pie is always sweet and sticky, deeply smooth on the tongue and delicious. The nuts are gracefully long and shapely, Georgia pecans, sunken in their caramel-colored, sugary, slightly crystalline sauce. They wash the pie down with long cold swallows of milk. Then, when they are done, they carry their trays to the window and hand them to food service workers, students like themselves, who are earning sixty-six cents an hour to help pay tuition or room and board (Joshua works in the education library three afternoons a week, also earning sixty-six cents an hour).

Then they cross the campus to the library, passing through the carved wooden doors (Joshua steps forward and holds the door open for Francie, who passes in front of him, aware of the powerful curve of his upper arm), and together they cross the marble floor, together they ascend the stairs to the long wood-paneled reading room, together they sit down, side by side, at one of the polished mahogany tables.

They begin their three hours of study: they open their books, open their notebooks, lay their pens and pencils in a row on the table. They read. They write. Francie is reading the works of Thomas Wolfe. Though the university owns certain original manuscripts of his, and though Francie requested the opportunity to examine them, she was refused. The rules would not allow her access: she was neither graduate student, nor scholar, nor male. But she has no use these days for rules that exclude her.

Despite what Liz may think of Wolfe, Francie loves his work. She will read *Look Homeward, Angel* again and learn how he writes the way he does. She and he have a special bond. Wolfe died exactly—to the day—six months after Francie was born. She believes, in some mysterious way, that she was meant to take his place in the literary cosmos. She loves his words from *Of Time and the River,* that writers write "to wreak . . . the rude and painful substance of his own experience into the . . . blazing and enchanted images that are themselves the core of life."

Francie, studying beside Joshua, has never been able to concentrate so well in her life. She feels as if she is floating outside of time, no longer restless, no longer seeking relief from the tedium of hard study, no longer needing to daydream, to let her glance linger on some boy across the table or across the room. She feels no pressure to stare at anyone or eavesdrop or leave her seat ten times in an evening to get a drink from the water fountain or comb her hair in the ladies' room.

This dutiful dedication to study is all in preparation for the reward that comes when she and Joshua leave the library. She doesn't allow herself even to imagine the coming moment: if she did, she would explode and fall earthward in a shower of fireworks. She would ignite all the students innocently studying around her, they and their books and paper, the vast holdings of the library itself, the rare books and manuscripts, the entire golden rows of the standing card catalog.

Holding off, waiting her turn, protecting all stored and bound historical knowledge from going up in smoke, Francie's bottom shivers on the hard wooden seat in anticipation of her own coming exquisite and ecstatic incineration.

# 17

# The Bench

If they arrive too early, before curfew begins in the dorms, a couple may already be under the tree. The protocol is delicate; they must approach slowly and with caution. Silence up ahead in the darkness is no indication of vacancy. They have made earlier mistakes, taking silence to mean the bench was empty when in fact lovers were using it.

One night she and Joshua were taken by surprise, deaf in the newness of their concentration, unconscious in their passion of holding, blind in their commotion of kissing, so that a warning cough, and the crackle of a twig was hardly alarm enough. The couple burst through the low hanging branches and stood right there in front of them, an intrusive and unwelcome vision.

She saw the girl's full skirt swirl away, the flash of a white crinoline beneath as she fled through the under-brush, the young man's low, embarrassed grunt of

"Oh, sorry!"—the sound of their feet crashing away through the leaves.

They were shaken for an hour afterward, Francie almost ready to announce she never wanted to come here again. But where else was there to go? Joshua lived in a rooming house full of students, she lived where she lived, they had no car, no money, no alternative.

At least she thanked the unknown compassionate campus architect who had arranged to install this one single bench in the heart of darkness, had chosen to create this island of privacy deeply hidden in a circle of low-hanging tree branches. The campus was filled with benches, benches along pathways, on the periphery of the dormitory gardens, lining the library walkway, on the edge of the miniature golf course, around the alligator's pen, but every one of them—except for this one—was a public bench, an easy-access bench, a bench with a view and also within view.

Their bench was not a secret. Word traveled, as it must, when something rare and precious exists. A hundred couples, perhaps a thousand couples, needed a place like this one. Of course, not all of them were limited to this most minimal accommodation; lovers were known to travel into the woods, to the Devil's Millhopper, out to a lake beyond the edge of town, even to use (as Francie well knew) the dormitory kitchen to find privacy.

The bench offered only primitive comfort that threatened extreme discomfort: it was freezing cold in winter, a buzzing mosquito swamp in damp weather. Now, in the spring, it was at its best, though its splintery boards tended to press shards of wood into a bared thigh or resting palm. Its hardwood was rock-hard to sit upon for hours. Furthermore, there was no bathroom, no running water, no cushion to recline on after love, when they desired only rest, when both body and soul yearned to sink into brief but complete peace and yearned (hopelessly) to sleep.

Francie and Joshua have arranged their present schedule to come here just after the library closes. They calculate their arrival at the bench just as curfew strikes in the dormitories. With the female population thus reduced, the bench becomes irrelevant. Francie's good luck is that she no longer lives in the dorms. Her freedom affords them this prime advantage.

⟨⟩

Tonight, they have blessed good fortune; it seems the bench is empty. Depending on the strength of moonlight, on the intensity of starlight, it takes their eyes some time to adjust, to see whether silence means no one is there or is just a pause in the small motions of figures who have already claimed their space. But no, stepping as warily as cougars, they sense no scent, see no motion, hear no heavy breathing or gasp of discovery. Joshua parts the canopy of branches as he might hold back a curtain to let her pass through. Then they are in their private bower. They put their books on the ground. He sits, holds open his arms, and she falls into them.

✻

What was it Mary Ella had said—"We girls are living right in the range of time all this is supposed to happen; it's nature's plan"? Could it be, then, that this pleasure, this joy, this surprising happiness they shared was merely nature's cold and canny seduction? Did Liz and Bill run off to Jacksonville to marry, and does Liz stand disconsolate at the window every evening because nature has a plan and they are nature's puppets? Pawns of the "biological imperative"? If this is true, then all pairing off would be random, as it was in sixth-grade dance class when the boys lined up on one side of the gym, the girls on the other, and—at the signal—each side had to walk directly forward and choose the person immediately opposite. (Even then, some veered, some walked out of line, some strode diagonally opposite to choose a partner who was, somehow, more right.)

If it were merely that Francie was "ripe," then why wouldn't Harvey Rubin have done? (Or would he have "done" if he'd come at Francie in the right way, with the right words?) Or any man in any of her classes? Or even one of her professors! And the twins, what a mystery! All those weeks, she was there, ripe, within their reach, in their house, her bedroom down the hall from theirs, her senses all aware, hungry for everything—yet it couldn't, and didn't, happen.

But, of course, none of the men she knew held their heads at the angle Joshua held his, none of them had his heavy-lidded dark eyes, none of them had his broad, beautiful hands or fingers that controlled the keys of a piano with such authority. None of them had his timbre of voice, or grace of movement; none had his sense of rootedness, or inward balance, or indifference to the opinions of others. What's more, none of them had ever looked at Francie the way he did, as if his eyes had just been opened, as if he had just come awake.

✳

They sit till the moon sets, till their teeth are chattering, their bodies shivering. How can they bear to part? Their hearts are pumping blood up to their ears, down to their toes; blood is pulsing in the sensitive flesh of their lips.

"We should go."

"Yes, we should go."

With her forefinger, she traces each of his fingers, as a child outlines her own hand with a pencil upon a sheet of drawing paper. To part is to embark on a desolate journey, long and intolerable, until morning, until they can meet for breakfast at the student union, take their doughnuts and coffee off to a corner of the room and stare at each other, lick the flakes of sugar from the corners of their mouths, sip from the steaming cups of coffee and let their tongues linger on the porcelain edges. Then another parting: the day's duties will wrench them from one another—propel them into their life in ordinary time. They must endure their classes and all that this entails, fulfill all their obligations to themselves and to the future, and only then can they come together on the bench, where time stops.

✳

One afternoon Liz comes into Francie's room. "I'm so glad this finally happened for you." She hangs onto one of the poles of the four-poster bed; her face is pale, her blond hair seems dimmed, not glowing with light as it used to. "You know, I've always been afraid that love could just as likely *not* happen as happen. The odds! The odds are so incredible that we could ever meet a person who answers our words with the right words. Who has a place in the curve under his neck that fits your head. A person that you want to be in the same room with forever. It's so unlikely, Francie, that every time it happens, the world should declare a miracle. Make a shrine to it."

"But, then, after the miracle happens—you suffer," Francie says. "Look how you're suffering. I've never seen you so sad."

"Because it's torture to be separated from him," Liz agrees. "Exquisite torture. I think it may actually kill me."

"But he calls you all the time," Francie says. "That must help."

"That makes it worse! It's something else that's killing me. I don't know if I should say it to you, Francie. Now that you're having something like it—though I don't know how far you two have gone—maybe you'll understand. But Francie, the thing is: once you've had sex, you want it again. You have to have it again or you'll die."

Francie doesn't know what to say, how much to admit. Liz has a gold band on her hand to justify her confession, but what should Francie say? That they've gone so far but no further? That they've done this much but not that? Are there even words to quantify where she and Joshua have been, in that other dimension, outside the bounds of ordinary time?

"You stay out so late, Francie. Where do you go? I know he doesn't have a car."

Francie can't just say: "The bench." She can't say a rough, common word that brings to mind a sitting place, where people place their behinds, where kids stop to tie their shoe laces, where women gossip. Their place behind the curtain of trees is as sacred as any temple, as private as a marriage bed.

"It's okay, you don't have to tell me." Liz says. "Look." She comes to Francie and puts her arms around her. "I always felt a little afraid of you before, but now, well, you've been initiated too, and you can understand. I'm afraid to talk to Amanda about this; she's so . . . chaste, you know. I don't know what's going on with her, I think she's in love with the twins. But who wouldn't be in love with the twins? We all were, weren't we?"

This is too much. Liz, who has barely spoken to Francie in all the weeks preceding, is asking too much now, going too far. Francie isn't willing to tell everything about Joshua. And the twins—it now seems they are artifacts from a former life of hers. They were her laboratory in which she practiced certain experiments, they were her blind study, a stand-in for whatever she was waiting for. Yes, she could see that she had practiced her longings on them, since they were so handy. But no—she hadn't loved the twins, now that she has felt what she has with Joshua.

"You never told me how you met him, Francie," Liz says. "You never said how this all got started so hot and fast. He *is* a beautiful man. But the speed of this, Francie!"

Yes. The fact is, she doesn't know how it happened so fast. When she tries to remember, she has only a sense of instantaneous combustion. A walk, a talk— and then he took her hand. In no time, they were living their bench-life. What was it Mary Ella had said: "Love strikes like a rattler"? Mary Ella, that prophet who held court on the mountaintop of her bed, the fortune-teller who sees all, knows all.

"I almost feel we're sisters now," Liz says. "Sisters in passion."

Francie gathers her books together. "I've got to go now, Liz. I have to meet Joshua. I'm glad we talked."

"But, listen—I may need your help," Liz says, "I'll tell you more about it later. The twins and I are going to concoct a way to get Bill out of basic training so that he can take a weekend's leave. A soldier can't leave basic training unless there's an emergency in his family, like a death or a suicide. I'm going to be one or the other—I just don't know yet which one!"

# 18

## *La Bohème*

Joshua has borrowed a car from one of the men who lives in his rooming house, and he and Francie are on their way north to Jacksonville for an evening at the opera. A traveling opera company is putting on *La Bohème,* which Joshua has explained will be a painless and appropriate introduction to opera for her. "It's about artists and art, about love and death," he told her last week—"It's about all the subjects you care about. It's made for you."

"It is?" So he knows her! She shivers with the thought that he has attended to her so carefully that he believes he already understands more about her—possibly—than she understands herself. After all, they have not talked half as much as they've simply clung to each other during these weeks of their connection; they have avoided putting thoughts of their future into hard-edged words lest all their hopes be talked into a clarity of impossibility.

What, after all, will happen to them after graduation? They will be separated and flung to the four corners of the earth. Certain wheels have been set in motion (long ago, long before she looked into the window of his practice room). He will be going to some graduate school, she to some unclear future. Unlike Mary Ella Root, she will not be engaged before graduation. She has not taken the requisite education courses to make her into an elementary school teacher. What next? What can she do other than type sixty words a minute? She wants to be a writer, an artist—and nothing in her education has supported her toward this goal. She, and all the women around her, have been encouraged only to be teachers, or perhaps nurses. And only if they haven't managed to find a husband.

She and Joshua are only half-formed, half-grown, not yet able to stand on their own in the world where adults create their own fates. Why can't they remain here, anchored in time where only this moment exists, where hard decisions are at bay?

Now the car speeds along the fragrant country road to the north. Joshua's profile is steady ballast against trees that whip past, their branches dragging with pointed raggedy beards of Spanish moss. If they drive just a little faster, the car will leave the road, take flight and ascend heavenward. Then they will be free. She imagines the two of them coming softly to rest in that dreamlike space lovers imagine for themselves: the desert island, the mountain top where no one can find them, the private paradise in some exotic and distant land. There they will have a bed instead of a bench; there they will have no work, no classes, no commitments. Why should there need to be a practical future when it would be far better to have just this man, this woman, and eternity ahead in which they might float in their adoration of each other?

But time ticks in them as in a bomb. The gas tank has only so much gas left before they must pull off the road and fill it up; the car is loaned only for this evening; the night is not endless. The opera will have its opening curtain—and in no time the curtain will come down. Francie wishes she did not foresee the end of everything so clearly. She is battered by foreknowledge.

✳

They take a mirrored elevator to the top level of the music hall. An usher guides them to their seats high in the balcony. Francie is wearing her best suit, stockings, little high heels, and Joshua looks striking in a dark suit, white shirt, and tie. Her breath always catches at the purity of his archetypal, square-jawed maleness, at his utter handsomeness. What's amazing is that he seems unaware of this, has none of the conceit of the cocky male, plays no games, offers up no seductive lines. Once, when they were studying side by side in the library, she asked him to draw a self-portrait of himself. He drew a little comic figure on his notebook paper, two round circles denoting a fat short fellow with big ears, big flat feet, and shoelaces trailing on the floor. "That's how you see yourself?" Francie had asked, and he'd replied, "Don't I look just like that?"

As Francie arranges her skirt, she has to look twice at whom she imagines she sees in the row just beneath them: Dr. Raskolnikov and the beautiful Frenchman Emil. What Francie recognizes first is the incomparable wavy hair of her Russian literature professor. Her reaction is to grip Joshua's hand till he whispers, "What's the matter? It this too high up for you? Are you dizzy?"

"I know those men," she whispers in his ear, indicating the seats below them. "My teacher and his friend."

"Want to say hello?" Joshua asks, and just then he must notice what Francie has already seen. In the dark hidden space between chairs, the two men are holding hands.

There is no way she can say hello. Francie wishes there were no balcony, no opera, no curtain just rising, no freezing garret, no Rodolpho, no Mimi, no Paris, no painters or poets or freezing snow. No Christmas. Her face is buried in the program. In the dim light from above, she reads the histories of the singers, where they took their educations, gave their early performances. Emil's blond curls and the professor's deep waves drown her. What she knows about love between people of the same sex is only this: when one summer during high school she worked posting monthly payments for a mortgage company, a woman in the firm often came to ask her some question or other. When she leaned over Francie's chair, she always put her hand delicately on Francie's shoulder. Her hand sometimes lingered there caressingly. At the time Francie felt a momentary discomfort but discounted it, ignored it each day it happened. Then one afternoon, in the ladies' room, a senior secretary warned her: "Let me tell you something about Lily. Don't let her near you. She's one of those . . . women, you know, who don't like men. Do you understand?"

Her first response was sympathy; *no one* liked the men who owned Kirschner Mortgage. Their bosses were large, overbearing brothers who smelled of cigar smoke, who wore large gold rings on their stubby fingers, who made off-color jokes about their wives and spent an inordinate amount of time giving dictation to Liza, the beautiful secretary of the office who had a husband away in the army; she laughed gaily when her buzzer rang. Time to take another letter. Time to disappear into the lushly carpeted office of one brother or another and to come out an hour later reeking of cigar smoke.

What Francie learned primarily at Kirschner Mortgage was that she never wanted to end up as a secretary. She never wanted to jump to the buzzer rung by a man.

Here, at the opera, there is no cigar smoke, but instead from the row below comes a whiff of fragrant cologne, with just a touch of something else beneath it, some dark bitter smell of alcohol.

✶

At the start of intermission, Francie sits with her head buried in the program until she is sure the men have disappeared up the aisle. Some cramping has started in her lower belly, the signal, she hopes, that her period is on the way. She has gone forty-eight days now. She's beginning to be concerned, though she's not sure why. She can't possibly be pregnant unless . . . no, that would be impossible.

"I'm going to the bathroom," she whispers to Joshua and leaves him to stumble uncertainly up the incline to find a rest room. A line of ladies is already in place along the edge of the red carpet. She takes her place among them. She is thinking about the unlikely nature of opera, in which ones sings one's deepest love and agonies, when she hears "Francie!"

Emil appears, beaming at her side. "What are you doing here?"

"Same as you, I guess," she says. The line is moving up and she can't lose her place.

"I must tell Leon you're here," he says. He flicks the edge of a green silk scarf around his neck.

"Oh, don't worry about it," she says. "Maybe he'd rather you didn't tell him you saw me."

"Francie," Emil says. He bends close to her ear. "You saw us at Leon's house. You know I live there with him. You aren't upset, knowing about us, are you?"

"Of course not," she says. "Why would I be?"

" You wouldn't. Because you have the soul of an artist," Emil says. "You understand life."

✳

In the ladies' room, Francie finds no omens or messages. When she returns to her seat, Professor Raskolnikov and Emil are gone. She stares at their empty seats.

"I think your friends may have moved down a few rows. Would you like to find some better seats, also?"

"Oh, no," Francie says. "Let's just stay right here."

# 19

# Gynecology

At day fifty-five, with no sign of blood, Francie finds herself standing in a public phone booth outside a drugstore on University Avenue with the phone book open to the section of the Yellow Pages headed "Physicians: Gynecologists." She chooses a name, Dr. Forster, a neutral name, almost generic, and dials. She can't believe she's doing this, but neither can she live one more night and day without knowing some facts, without having some relief. This can't be happening to her, a virgin by all technical definitions, a girl with a head on her shoulders, a good student, who has kept calendars of her menstrual history since she was thirteen. As her mother had instructed her at the beginning of her fertile life, she must write the initials "D.C." on the calendar precisely on the day her period was expected (twenty-eight days from the last one), and then, when her "Delicate Condition" arrived, she must place a check mark at the date. Her range of variation has been small, from twenty-seven days to thirty-one, quite consistently since the day at Girl Scout camp when she first found the herald on her cotton underpants. Now, fifty-five days between delicate conditions produces in her soul pure panic.

"Could I speak to Dr. Forster, please?" Francie says to the woman who answers the phone, a nurse or receptionist.

"May I tell him who's calling?"

"I'm not his patient," Francie says, "but I have something very important I need to know." Her voice cracks, and, to her astonishment, she begins to cry.

"Oh, my! Hang on, dear. I'll see what I can do, just a moment." Francie hangs on, waiting, at a public phone in a public place, astonished that she could ever have come to such a pass in life.

"Hello. This is Dr. Forster. Is there some way I can help you?" The doctor's voice is strong, capable; she wants to sink into his arms and sob her heart out.

"You don't know me, and I don't know how to ask you this," she says, "but my period is very late, and I need to know, if a person doesn't have intercourse, can she . . . can a woman still get pregnant?"

"How old are you, my dear?"

"Twenty-one."

"And what exactly happened, if you can tell me?"

My boyfriend . . . I mean, we were sitting very close. . . ." She has an image of the bench, the darkness under the tree, herself sitting sideways across Joshua's lap, her arms around his neck, the cold wind, the feel of his mouth pressed hard against her lips, and his sudden quivering under her, the iron grip of his arms till the spasm released him. She'd stood up quickly, at once, not to reject him but to protect herself, feeling that back of her skirt was wet. It was not the first time they'd had to sit on the bench a long while, till the dark mark on his pants faded, dried in the wind, making it possible for him to go back to his rooming house. But on this night her skirt was silken-thin, it took his fluid like a sponge, passed it through her nylon panties. Could this mere dampness, this fluid thick with the stuff of procreation, have somehow gotten to the hidden place within her where life starts?

"Sperm, you know, they are determined little fellows," Dr. Forster says. "They can be pretty spunky. I wish I could tell you it's impossible, but sperm are very tenacious. It's not likely, you know, but it has been known to happen."

"Then I could be . . . ?"

"How many days?"

"Fifty-five."

There is a long pause while she waits, while she supposes the doctor is making his learned calculation. He says, finally, "Don't you do anything drastic, young lady. It may be nothing at all. Why don't you come and see me in a few days if things don't change? We will keep it confidential, of course."

"Oh, thank you," Francie says.

"You won't do anything not sensible, will you? I want you to assure me of that."

What could he mean? Her knees are too weak to hold her up. "I won't," she says. She hangs up and stumbles down the street till she finds a bench, a bench in bright daylight, under no tree, and falls upon it till she can get her bearings.

✴

That night, while she and Joshua are studying in the library, she contemplates how she will tell him about this. She doesn't know how to say the words, that when they were together she got wet, that the wetness was not dew or mist but the terrifying milky fluid of life itself. Would he take it as a criticism, implying lack of control or caution? Surely, neither trait can be fairly assigned to him. He has—from the beginning—been nothing if not a gentleman. He has never pressed her to go further in their delicate bench maneuvers than those acts to which she has wholeheartedly agreed. Never for a moment had she felt shame in his presence, but only approval, appreciation, encouragement to go deeper with him into this new country they have been exploring together.

What if the worst were true? That she was indeed pregnant? What would they do?

She brings herself back to the present, to the murmuring library environment, where if she closes her eyes she can hear the turning of notebook pages all around her, the scratch of pens on paper, the hum of low voices, the sliding on polished grooves of the drawers of the card catalog.

Joshua, beside her, is studying philosophy. She, with her biography of Tolstoy open on the table before her (her final term paper in Dr. Raskolnikov's class is titled "Tolstoy's Attitude toward Women"), studies Joshua.

What does he mean to do with her now that she is his? Where is he going next, and will he take her with him? He seems unconcerned about such matters, he deflects discussions of his future plans, doesn't speak of their conjoined fate, behaves as if there is only this night, this moment, and perhaps tomorrow morning. His sense of responsibility toward the future seems to have no place for her. Awaiting him are graduate school, military service, things to be accomplished, gotten out of the way, tended to before his own personal desires can even be examined. Eons have to pass before he can be an adult with an adult life. As for Francie and her own future, she has nothing she wishes for but somehow, if the fates will grant her enough talent, to be a writer. That and always to be part of Joshua. They do not seem contradictory desires.

In her room, sometimes, she secretly leafs through Mary Ella's *Bride's* magazine, desiring finally the thing she had scorned, not the fifteen bridesmaids and the crystal goblets, not the gown of satin and pearls, not the long taffeta train or the floral arrangements, not the darling children who act as ring bearers—but the ring! She wants only to have the ring, the simplest of gold bands, like the ring on Liz's finger that guarantees her a place to be, and someone to belong to. Like all the other girls she knows, she has caught this virus, this overpowering need to connect, this ultimate requirement.

Joshua, beside her, studies on. His total absorption in work irritates her. She glances at the page he is taking into his powerful mind and sees words that are vague and overblown: "existence of God," "meaning of life," "moral certainty," "utopian principles."

The meaning of life! She could have his child inside her! This is her certainty, her terror, her ecstasy. Next to that, arguments about the existence of God are utter nonsense.

✳

When the library lights dim to warn that it is nearly closing time, she and Joshua gather their books under their arms and walk, automatically, in the direction of the bench.

When they are nearly there, Francie digs in her feet like a mule. "I don't want to go to the bench," she says. "I want to talk to you."

"Can't we talk there?" He smiles at her in a way that makes her heart contract with guilt. He never seems to imagine how she seethes with her private resentments and longings. If they have been in the library studying, he—guileless—imagines that she, like he, has been studying. How can he assume that all is as it seems, that all is right with the world and will continue to be? Is this a man's gift, or blessing, for him to take things as they are, or to assume they will work out? Not to imagine calamity, or worry, or invent dread scenarios? Are men, in general, that stupid? That trusting? That unimaginative?

She suggests that they go to the bar where Harvey Rubin took her. "We could drown our troubles," she says. "We could have a beer."

"Do you like beer?" Joshua asks. He stares at her, as if trying to integrate this possibility into all he knows of her.

"Sometimes," she says, cruelly, untruthfully. "At least there won't be mosquitoes there."

Though he is clearly disappointed, he agrees, and they walk without speaking to the campus gathering place and find their way to a booth. When they have ordered (both order Cokes, not beers), while he is sipping from his straw, Francie tells Joshua that her period is almost a month late.

He waits for her to continue, his eyebrows raised. He doesn't understand.

"I could be pregnant," she whispers across the table.

"But you know that's not possible," he says. "I mean—how?" He waits. He looks into her eyes. Does he think she's going to confess she has another lover?

"It is possible. I even called a doctor to ask if it could be."

"How could it be? We never . . . we didn't even . . ."

"The fluid. Sperm swim," she says. "They're tricky."

"Oh!" Joshua reaches over the table and takes her hand. He smiles into her eyes. "That would be like a comet coming through the roof and landing on our table, Francie. I knew a girl in high school who was worried about that; she thought that maybe while she was swimming that could happen, that she could be . . . but of course it didn't come to anything at all."

"A girl in high school? Was she your girlfriend?"

"I'd hardly call her that."

"But you were her friend?"

"I guess you could say so. We both worked together one summer at a hotel on Miami Beach."

"So you were swimming with her when something happened?" The words shoot out of Francie's mouth. She feels as if her eyes are floodlights in an interrogation room. Joshua looks away from her, to the lit beer signs on the walls, to the couples in booths around the room.

"Well?"

"She thought something happened."

Francie's eyes feel as if acid has been thrown at them; color fades from the room. She didn't expect this twist, this overlay of one torment upon another. How stupid she has been to think the passion they share is as new an experience for him as it is for her. She feels a sickness in every cell of her body.

156

"Excuse me," she says, rising quickly from the table. "I feel sick."

✳

She comes back a long while later and stands at their table. He is pale now, his face full of alarm. He rises and puts his arm around her shoulders. "What's wrong, Francie? Do you think you can walk home?"

She lets him think whatever he may be thinking. Let him be afraid, let him think her nausea is a sign of the impossible threat. He has, after all, betrayed her with some high school girl. Oh, he truly disgusts her, he with his manly beautiful arms, his square jaw, his sweet smile. He with his gentle humor, his integrity. My God. Is there no end to what her mind will do to wreck her peace? This jealousy is insane, she knows it, but it's eating her alive.

Joshua's face is dark with concern as they leave the bar. He carries her books, lets her lean on his shoulder as they walk toward her house. Her breath is foul in her mouth, she is going to die of grief. He has been aroused by someone else, some woman not her, and thus has become a monster. How can this man beside her be looking at her with tender worry, be smiling assurances into her eyes? Doesn't he understand she is now dead, and he is death's messenger?

# 20

## Collusion

Francie?"

Liz taps on her door late at night. Francie is in bed, under the covers.

"How are you feeling now? Do you want a heating pad? I have some codeine if you need it."

Francie can't talk; she flings herself about on the bed. The pain is grinding, without pause.

"Breathe through your mouth; it makes you relax." Coming into the room, Liz sits at the foot of the bed and touches Francie's leg. "Don't you just love the privilege of being a woman? My mother used to tell me to think of my cramps as a blessing, God's way of reminding me about the glory of creation. But *every* month? Wouldn't a reminder once a year, say, be quite sufficient?"

Francie grunts. She can't turn philosophical just

now, not in the grip of this wrenching corkscrew of pain.

"I'm never having children," Liz confides. "Does the world really need more of us illustrious, brilliant, angelic human beings? Aren't there enough kids around by now to cover all the bases? Besides, why would one of my kids be any more likely to be a Shakespeare than one of the thirteen kids that belong to the janitor who cleans Peabody Hall? And even if I had a guarantee that I'd produce a genius, is another Shakespeare really needed?" Liz asks. "Remember—even he wondered if life was worth the struggle—'to be or not to be,' right?—where did all that talent and genius get Shakespeare? He's just as dead as anyone. He understood everything and he died anyway. So what's the point?"

Francie sighs. She's so tired. If only the pain would stop, she could sleep.

"Immortality is worth zero, Francie. Do you think posterity is going to write you a thank you note for what you leave behind? Remember in *To the Lighthouse,* Francie? Remember when Virginia Woolf has Mr. Bankes say, 'Why does one take all these pains for the human race to go on? Is it so very desirable? Are we attractive as a species?' 'Not so very,' he says. I know this because I just wrote about that in my term paper. Immortality is cold comfort, Francie. We'd better be happy and have fun while we're right here, Francie. In the here and now."

"Oh God," Francie moans. "The here and now."

"I'll get off my soapbox," Liz says. "I'm sorry; just seeing you this way carried me away. And you're not even having a baby, so this is all academic, isn't it."

A baby! If Liz had any idea! If Liz could even guess how overjoyed Francie is not to be having a baby!

"Tea?" Liz asks. "A nice warm cup of tea? With lots of sugar?"

"Yes—thanks, Liz. But, excuse me—I'll be right back." She struggles out of bed and staggers to the bathroom. Her sanitary napkin, the mysterious screen on which she has been watching for her future to unfold, contains—along with her menstrual blood—thick black clots, irregular formations, mysterious, twisted designs of tissue. Finally, the blood of deliverance has made its showing, has delivered her from her terror. Could it be that these tiny pieces of matter are parts of a potential genius? Of her child? Fortunately, she will never know. What she does know is that she is pardoned from the shame of having to visit Dr. Forster, of having to face the closing down of her future, of having to accuse Joshua of contributing to her ruination. She is excused from having to fly to Puerto Rico to have an abortion. She knows of a girl who was forced to do this and came back with her insides in ribbons.

This mere pain! What of it? It is nothing. She relishes it, she cherishes it. Her pain is her freedom. She can go her way now, Joshua can go his way—if that's his choice. His record is pristine; he's saved from admitting any wrongdoing. Saved from his moral responsibility. Francie and that foolish, frightened high school friend of Joshua's who swam with him in the pool, the girl who swam dangerously close to him, were worriers for nothing. A mere clog in the lunar clock was the cause of all this female hysteria. Much ado about nothing!

Then why does Francie still carry this monumental anger? Where does this level of jealousy come from? How could she mind that Joshua once had some primal response to another female? Would Francie have wanted him—when he didn't even know she existed— to have been sexless, blank, uninterested in women, uninterested in the exploration of his own powerful male instincts?

Good God! She's losing her mind. She has been pressed to the edge of terror by the fear that she might be pregnant, and now—knowing that she is not—she is flooded with anger that Joshua did not understand this fear, made light of it, had not the slightest sense of how many times in the last weeks she had rushed into various bathrooms to check her underpants, wept into her hands for fear of what would become of her if she were that shameful forbidden thing—pregnant! What worse fate could befall an unmarried girl? Just the thought of her parents' horrified faces had they heard such news brings her now to a burst of tears. She has almost disgraced them all! She knew better! She should not have done those things, in that way, on that bench. She did them for pleasure, out of selfish need and hunger. She did them because she wanted to do them. Good girls, as everyone knew, waited till they were married. Therefore, it is clear, she is not good.

All right. It is settled then, she knows what is.

✶

"So let me tell you our plan now that you're feeling a little better," Liz says to Francie as they sip tea. Francie is back in bed; Liz is sitting on the old rocking chair in the bedroom. "We know it's risky, but the thing is, I'm willing to do anything to get Bill free from the army for the weekend. Otherwise, oh God, I won't be able to see him for weeks yet."

Francie takes slow, deep breaths. The hot tea and Liz's codeine pill have reduced the force of the gripping, grinding sensation in her gut. The familiar sensation of ache in her pelvis and at the back of her knees now seems to resemble what she always feels during a regular menstrual period.

"What plan are you talking about?"

"Well, for one thing, we figured out the perfect place to meet Bill. The twins' parents own a cabin at Peachtree Lake that's just over the Georgia border. There's a motorboat there and a dock and fishing, and it's gorgeous in the woods now that it's spring. The lake may even be warm enough to swim in. The twins' parents never use the cabin now, so that's not a problem; they won't turn up. The best thing, of course, is that the lake is near the base where Bill is stationed; if he can get leave, he can take a Greyhound bus and be there in a couple of hours. The only thing is, I need to ask you to do a huge, major, enormous favor for me."

"Like what?" Francie asks. She is feeling slightly dizzy now.

"All you have to do is pretend you're my psychiatrist."

"Oh, really? Oh, sure. That's all?" She laughs. She is so surprised that she is able to laugh that she laughs again. "Well, why not?" she says, thinking that no risk can be as great as the one she just escaped from.

"You just have to say you're calling from the Student Health Center. Amanda could never carry it off; she's too honest, and her voice would shake. The twins would probably try it, but they'd just start laughing if they made the call. You're the only one I can really trust."

"How come?"

"You're brave, Francie. You have that steely side to you . . . like I have. That's why I think you could do it for me. You'd just call Bill's army base. You would ask for his commanding officer and tell him that Bill's wife—that's me—is suicidally depressed. That you've been counseling her. That she might actually try something like jumping off the bell tower. She desperately needs to see him. That's all. Then they'll have to give him emergency leave for the weekend."

"They'll have to?"

"It's their policy, for a death in the family or a

horrendous crisis—that sort of thing. Then he can meet us at Peachtree Lake, and we'll have a party!"

"But what if they ask questions about your condition?"

"I have it all written out. You'll say I've been depressed since Bill left, and now my father is dying in Istanbul of some dread disease (my mother is already an alcoholic, so I can't go home to stay with her), and I'm clearly suicidal—and you're my psychiatrist and you believe that only a visit from my husband could turn this around and save my life. That's all there is to it. Then, when they say okay, we all pile in the car and zoom out to the lake, and Bill meets us there. We'll have fun, Francie! In the here and now!"

Indeed—Francie would like to have fun. "I was going to study this weekend," she says, "but so what?" Now that she knows for certain she's not a good girl, this challenge seems appropriate for her. She'll lie—so what?

"It doesn't matter if you don't study. By this point, we all know we're going to graduate. But are you worried about leaving Joshua?"

"No, not at all!" Francie says. She's surprised at the venom in her voice. "He's so sure of me—it might do him good if I just disappeared for a whole weekend." Suddenly, the plan seems like a brilliant idea. Let him imagine she's run off with a football hero! Let him feel something like the jealousy that has so painfully consumed her. Why not let him suffer? Women always suffer! They wait for men to call and then wait for men to call them back. Women wait for proposals and wait for marriage. Women wait for their periods. Women writhe with cramps every month, and women bear the children.

Let Joshua wait. Let Joshua writhe. Let a man suffer for once.

# 21

# Peachtree Lake

*T*he woods are lovely, dark and deep . . . "
Indeed, they are, as the five of them fly along the road to Peachtree Lake in Georgia. All hurdles have been conquered, all aims achieved. Francie is astonished that she has been able to deceive the United States Army. How easy, she discovered, it is to lie, to bear a calculated indifference to truth, country, flag, and immortal soul. Liz's fictional suicidal state started the party going, and Francie has made it real by her stunningly successful phone call. Bill was given immediate emergency leave and is already on his way to the lake. He and his happy housemates are going to party in the woods all weekend.

And all this without a word to Joshua. Francie's recent fear of pregnancy, her jealousy of the unknown high school girl who aroused Joshua's sexual excitement, her desperation about her need for Joshua to commit his love forever, all these have somehow disgusted her. She wants time off from these damaging thoughts. She wants to defuse—to *refuse*—the panic she's caught about graduating without the proverbial promise of an MRS degree. These last weeks have brought some new clarity to Francie's mind—as if she's stepped over a line into another country. Now she lets the wind stir her hair and feels the hot breeze of the Georgia countryside swirl past her face. They'll soon be there, physically, in that other country.

She thinks about the Robert Frost poem that keeps repeating in her mind, and how she heard the poet himself read it to audience of students one night last fall in the university auditorium, Frost a great, round-shouldered, wild-haired old man who knew everything about life. He had lived with his wife in Gainesville for many years before her death. How his white hair caught the stage lights and sent flashes of beauty into Francie's head as he read his poem:

> *"The woods are lovely, dark and deep*
> *but I have promises to keep*
> *And miles to go before I sleep"*

She had bought his book of poems and stood in line for him to sign it.

When it was her turn, as he wrote the letters of his name in a shaky hand on the title page of his book, she shyly confessed to him, "I hope to be a writer, too."

He looked up, and his blue eyes burned into hers. "Good," he said. "It's the right thing to do if you have the calling."

✳

"Be sure to watch out for stinging nettles, Francie."

Liz, holding her guitar in her arms as if it is an unwieldy child, stands on the porch of the cabin while Francie picks her way along the overgrown path. The twins and Amanda are behind Francie, unloading boxes of supplies from the car parked on the road.

"What does a stinging nettle look like?"

"Sometimes you say words so *weird*," yells one of the twins from the road. "The way you say 'neh-ul' and the way you say 'boh-ul,' too. Even 'tur-ul'—I get a kick out of you when you do that."

"It's New Yorkese," Liz explains to the twin. "Bill talks like that, too. They call it a glottal stop, I think."

But Francie is astonished; for one thing, a twin has taken notice of her. For another, that he has just said he "gets a kick out of her," when he has never paid her any attention at all, ever. She doesn't know which twin he is, Jerry or Bobby—she has forever given up trying to make the distinction. She truly doubts the boys' own mother could tell them apart.

She pauses on the path, taking in the smell of trees, flowers, and berries. The scent of pine bark is hot in the sun. Beyond the cabin, the lake sparkles and glints. Under the fragrance of blossom and grass is a rank odor

Francie can't identify. She lifts her head and inhales deeply.

"Duck shit," the twin behind her says accommodatingly. "There's nothing you can do about it. Over at the landing, where everyone swims, the ducks keep pretty clear of that, but over here, at the shore, they do stink. You get used to it after a while."

Amanda and the twin speaking to Francie are coming up from the car with their overnight cases, a cooler, some books. *I'm in Georgia,* Francie thinks. In her writing class they read the amazing stories of Flannery O'Connor, who lived on a peacock farm with her mother. Now she looks around, wondering if she will see a Bible salesman or an escaped convict. At the moment, she considers that she is a misfit herself, a morally bereft sinner whose soul is lost for eternity. Like Hulga in *Good Country People,* she is too smart for everyone, yet full of failings and base desires. She wonders at her transformation from the good girl who roomed with Mary Ella Root just a few months ago to this wild woman who last week placed an anonymous call to a gynecologist, who yesterday called the United States Army and pretended to be a psychiatrist at the Health Center who was treating Liz for depression. She, furthermore, has deceived her parents, who do not know she has been living in a house with men. She has disappeared into the Georgia woods without even telling the man she loves that she is going away.

Amanda, from the looks of things, may be finding

herself in the same circumstances, a good girl set free from the Church of Good Girls. She's wearing a devil-may-care orange sundress and white sandals. Her loose blonde hair is blowing wildly in the breeze. "I'm not even going to try to study," she calls into the wind. "I don't care if I don't graduate. Who wants to graduate if I have to go off to teach second grade somewhere?"

"Not I," calls Liz gleefully.

"Not I," Francie agrees.

"Not I!" Amanda shouts.

"What is this, 'The Little Red Hen'?" Liz demands of them, still laughing.

"My mother told me last week that I've failed hopelessly in my mission. At least if I were engaged to be married, I would have accomplished something. That's what college was for, as far as she's concerned." Amanda throws up her arms. "So I've wasted all that tuition."

"Well I *just* managed to get a man," Liz says. "By the skin of my teeth. I almost didn't make it!"

The twins are silent; they don't seem to know what to make of this display of female craziness. The two of them stand on the porch, shoulder to shoulder, like cut-out dolls made from the same design on a sheet of paper and unfolded into two.

They leave the girls shouting nonsense into the wilderness and enter the cabin. Francie can see after them through the open front door and right out the back windows to the lake. It's so very beautiful here in this late afternoon light, so still, so hot and alive with the sounds of birds and crickets and the buzz of bees.

"Let's figure out where we'll sleep," Liz says, leading them into the house.

One of the twins is turning on the refrigerator motor. "You and Bill will get the real bedroom, the one my parents always use," he says. "It's only right when Bill gets here you two should have some privacy. Then Amanda and Francie can have the room we always slept in when we were kids, and we two will sleep on the couches in the living room."

Francie is amazed at all these words flying about. After the weeks of silence in the house in town, some lid has been taken off—all of them are talking as if they had just learned how to use words. They're all giddy.

"Let's get some of this stuff in the refrigerator," Liz says. "I'll put the roast in to cook, and then we can take a walk. Maybe go around the lake. When we come back, we'll pick up Bill at the bus station. And then we'll celebrate. Feast! Drink wine! A night of revels!"

"This is so scary," Amanda says. "Do you think we can get away with it?"

"We already have!" Liz says. "We're here, we did it."

Out on the lake, through the window in the tiny bedroom where she's put her overnight bag, Francie can see a little group of ducks paddling along. How regal and graceful they are, gliding by, the iridescent feathers on their necks shimmering in rainbow colors. But underneath, there's that stench.

In the kitchen, she helps Liz put the milk and bacon and eggs into the refrigerator, which is just beginning to turn cool. There's an old-fashioned toaster on the wooden kitchen table, of the sort that doesn't pop up. The stove has quaint porcelain handles and black wrought iron grates over the burners.

"This stuff is from prehistory," Liz says. Amanda is unpacking a bread, a box of doughnuts, bags of potato chips and cookies. "This really is like a dream," she says. "From that stuffy old library, from memorizing the causes of the Civil War, to—total paradise!"

✱

Something has changed here. Romance—or a kind of guilty desire—is in the air. Perhaps the knowledge that Bill is coming to reclaim his bride makes those who are unpaired feel required to pair up. As they walk along the path that circles the lake, one twin walks with Amanda, one with Francie. Liz dances ahead, buoyant as a sunbeam, hopping and skipping, looking ten years old in her white shorts and yellow halter top. The twin at Francie's side reaches over to take her arm and guide her around some tree roots on the path. When they have negotiated the obstacle, he continues to hold her arm for a minute or two longer. Both twins are dressed in blue jeans and blue work shirts. They seem thinner, taller, and more angular than ever. Their shapes appear to Francie more foreign than usual. She has got used to Joshua's dimensions, to his mature, manly measurements. His center of gravity is lower than the twins', his arms are more muscular, his shoulders broader, his hair darker and thicker. His face, when unshaven, has a darker growth of beard than the twins', who are so fair.

She compares male qualities and feels astonishment that once she had wished to surrender herself (could she *ever* have wished this?) to one of the twins. As she thinks this, almost at the instant she thinks this, the twin beside her takes her hand. It could be a mere extension of his act of helping her around the tricky tree roots; it could be an automatic act of hand holding, in the way that a parent takes the hand of a child while crossing a dangerous street. But here she is, hand in hand with one of the tall, handsome, sandy-haired, inscrutable twins. His hand is cool and loose, long-fingered, almost bony in hers. But his grip is strong and forceful. She glances at him quickly, sideways, and then stares forward on the path. Up ahead is another cabin, and beyond that is the landing, where she can see a wooden pier, a sandy beach, and some people on blankets. She sees, also, the gentle lap of lake water rolling onto the shore.

She dares not turn around yet, but, when she can, she checks to see what's happening behind her. A quick turn of her head confirms her suspicion. Amanda and the other twin are also hand in hand! Is this a conspiracy, a plot? Has it all been worked out in advance? And, if so, by whom? Could Liz have conspired with them? Or is it a process of natural selection? With Liz taken (and of course the twins have forever been in love with Liz), and with Liz about to be claimed tonight by her rightful mate, then does logic call for the twins to make do with the available females? And is one as good as the other? Did the twins toss coins for who would get Francie and who would get Amanda? (Do the twins know anything about Joshua? They are so dense, maybe not. Maybe they have not even noticed Francie's recent late hours, her absence from the house.)

"There's our old motor boat," the twin walking with Amanda calls out. "Let's see if it starts up. Then we can all ride around the lake."

✳

While the boys abandon the girls to inspect their favorite of all things in a world, a grease-covered motor, Liz and Francie and Amanda sit on the edge of the pier, kicking their feet above the scummy water. Liz has high color on her cheekbones as if she has applied rouge too forcefully; she seems rosy and heated, burning with anticipation.

What of Amanda? She's so private, quiet, so reluctant to oppose Liz in any way—and is she, like Francie, worried about the coming night? It's bound to present difficulties. Who will make the first move, and what will it be, and how will they handle it?

Francie knows she could use this night to even the score with Joshua; she could do with one of the twins whatever it was Joshua did with that high school girl in a pool. What was it, exactly? She knows of girls who did many things with many men—and didn't die of it.

She knows a girl who lived in her dormitory, a girl who signed out on weekends, stating she was staying with an aunt in Ocala but instead going to live in the woods with her sociology professor. She was small and plain, wore glasses, was not pretty. But each weekend she went away, and each Sunday night she returned, calmly, full of a peaceful superiority, knowing what she knew, remembering what she had done.

This is a new world here. Francie shivers; the smell of duck leavings is potent, dark, almost nauseating. The boys have had some success with the motorboat. They have gotten in it now, and are *put-putting* toward the dock.

"Come on in," they cry together. They pull up under the six legs of the girls and reach up to seize their thighs. "We'll help you in."

✳

Liz declines. She will walk back to the cabin, check on the roast, put together a salad, take a little rest. She's tired. Much has happened already today, and much more will happen tonight. She waves them off—have a nice ride. Come back in an hour—then it will be time to pick up Bill at the bus station!

She sets off along the path, a small delicate figure glowing in the light of sunset. Francie feels herself lifted bodily off the splintery boards of the dock, held by the hips between the strong hands of a twin as he lowers her to the shuddering, rocking floor of the motor

# 22

# Terror

"atch this!"

Francie holds on to the side of the little boat and prays. When boys say "Watch this," they are beyond recall. In her childhood, she watched boys walk on the ledges of tall buildings, saw boys hang out of eighth-floor apartment house windows, observed boys reading dirty comics hidden in their history books at school. In high school, she saw boys in fast cars race other boys almost to the death, saw boys chug-a-lug whole bottles of whiskey without taking a single breath, and saw boys—on a dare—shoplift lacy lingerie from the local department store.

Here, on Peachtree Lake, these man-boys have the look of the devil on their faces. One twin, who controls the outboard motor, is sitting behind the wooden seat where Francie and Amanda are balanced. The other twin faces them from where he sits in the pointy end of the boat. His knees seem as high as his face. The two of them are grinning at each other the way boys grin when they hang out of high windows.

"Here goes!"

The boat jolts out into open water and buzzes beneath them as it picks up speed. The oily scum parts and floats out in rainbow waves as they tear forward toward the pine-green horizon. Amanda grasps Francie's hand; the two of them hang on for dear life.

So: this is the famed life of thrills! This is wildness! This is what losing control is about. Here in the South, the decadent, gothic South of Francie's literature classes, is where anything can happen—the South where, in Faulkner's story "A Rose for Miss Emily," the shunned spinster murders the Yankee who refuses to marry her and then keeps his dead body in her bed for forty years and sleeps beside it. This is the part of the world where, in O'Connor's story, a Bible salesman seduces an unhappy, unmarriageable girl into a barn loft and then disconnects and steals her wooden leg as part of his seduction. (He puts it in his Bible case with his collection of glass eyes and other artificial body parts stolen from women.)

*Let me experience all of life's thrills!* Francie wants to beg the gods. *Let me let go of caution!*

But in fact she and Amanda are eager to live. They scream. They cry out. They beg the twins to slow down.

There is a leaden thump every time the bow of the boat leaps out of the water and falls back down, a painful slap in the gut before the next wave comes to greet them.

The wind flails their hair against their faces and pricks their eyes with it. The twins are like boatmen on the River Styx, guarding them before and aft, ferrying them into hell. Francie begins to anticipate each thud and vibration, rising and falling with the boat's rhythm until she almost begins to look forward to the repetition, almost feeling pleasure from the regularity of the whipping shudder.

But finally the fury subsides, the pace lessens, the motor modulates from a roar to a growl to an even purr, then to silence. They have come to the opposite shore; they are floating slowly under an overhang of trees.

"How about that?" The twins, having made wild speed happen out of metal parts, motor oil, and gasoline, are in their element.

"It's got a great little engine, doesn't it?" They nod and agree, almost awestruck, praising their motor as one might praise God.

Francie and Amanda look around. The sun is low, darkness is settling upon the deep. There's a hint of chill in the shadowed place under the trees. What if the motor will not start again? What if they are actually stranded here? Francie looks to see if there are oars in the boat. There are not. She sees only a rusted tin can and some rope under a seat. She could never swim across the lake. She wants to ask these questions, but she cannot.

She suddenly remembers a moment in time when she was a child. Her father's car had had a flat tire. Her father was kneeling in the road, in the dark, asking her mother to direct a flashlight at the wheel, just a simple thing, so that he could see where to unscrew the bolts. Her mother pelted him with questions: "What if you can't unscrew the tire? What if the spare tire doesn't fit? What if someone comes along and holds us up? What if the batteries go dead in the flashlight? What if it gets cold? What if it rains? What if we never get out of here?" The real question, Francie knew, was "What if we die?" And finally her father smacked the fender of the car with his fist, in a fury. "Just hold the light," he said to Francie's mother. "Just hold the light."

✳

Francie sits, exercising calmness, her hands folded in her lap. She breathes deeply and looks around. The lake is vast, losing color and light. She watches the sun leave Amanda's golden hair, bit by bit, till her hair is the color of sand, then seaweed, then rock. The twins are still, each at his end of the boat, in some kind of trance. One of them says, "I'm thinking of the Roach brothers."

"When we lost our bet with them."

"Those boys."

"About that night their father wanted to roast the pig."

"First they had to kill it."

"Didn't want to."

"But their father said they had to. . . ."

"And collect the blood—"

"Our mother, though—"

"She said don't go—"

"But we went."

"Yeah . . . we went."

"Sure did."

"I'm glad we did."

"I don't say glad."

"We wouldn't have missed it, though."

"No, glad we saw it."

Francie stares at the long legs of the twin in front of her, his stork legs, his knees relaxed now, his legs spread out in a wide V, his knees now touching the two sides of the boat.

Who are these boys, and how did she fall into their power? There's something in them nonverbal and deep as the lake. What did they know? What did they share? What kind of a bond was it, to be a twin, to have the same shape and smell, the same face, the same eyes, the same mind as someone else?

Even Amanda, sitting meekly beside Francie, is deep inside her own pretty skull, knowing this moment the way she is fated to know it, different from the twins' way, different from Francie's way. Francie will never know what it is like in another mind. Never, no matter how long she knows a man or a woman, no matter how much she loves a person, or how much he tries to tell her of his private soul, will she ever know anything but her own tiny thoughts.

She shivers.

The twin behind her puts a warm, heavy hand on her shoulder.

"You cold," he says. It's not a question.

Francie nods, turning to look over her shoulder at him.

"Night falls fast this time of year," he says. She feels him stand up, and the boat tilts beneath his shifting weight.

"Hang on," he says, and she feels him give a pull on the motor cord. She waits with him and feels him wrench it again. Amanda squeezes her hand on the seat between them. Francie looks down at her feet, which she can hardly see now. He pulls again. Again. Again. Again.

"Want me to give it a try?"

"Give it a try."

The twins change places, stepping, it seems, over the heads of Francie and Amanda. There's much rocking and tilting, splashing of water against the sides, the sense of going over. The boat balancing out in flatness again.

The twin now in the captain's seat makes his try. The grating pull, rough and fierce, rends the air. And again. Again. Again.

"Shit."

"That's what you get for trusting an old piece of junk."

"It's froze up."

"Or out of gas."

"We can wait a while. Try again."

Francie has to clap her hands over her mouth in order not to say it: What if we never get back? What if we starve here? Freeze here? What if we die? Then she tells herself: *Just hold the light.*

✳

It is certain now something is seriously wrong. Maybe they will actually die here. Amanda is shivering beside her. Lights have come on in the houses across the lake. On their side of the lake there is only darkness—trees and wilderness.

"I'll swim over and see if Bailey's there. Then I'll come back in his boat to get you."

The other twin, his hand still on Francie's shoulder, says, "I'll go with you."

"Don't both go!" Amanda begs.

"It's better that way," the twins say at the same time. One of them adds, "If Bailey isn't there, we can take his boat anyway, get some gas for the outboard, come back for you. Then one of us can bring in this old tub if we can start it up."

Francie knows this is a plan that will take a century . . . and they will be left here to wait out the hundred years. The questions of catastrophe lie on her tongue like rancid oil.

"Okay, then, so we'll see you soon."

She feels the boat rock as the boys, in front of and behind her, unzip their jeans, step out of their pants, pull off their shirts.

"We're strong swimmers," the twin behind her bends down and says into Francie's ear. She feels something brush the top of her head—the reassuring pat of his hand. A farewell touch.

"Hey, we know this lake inside out," the other twin says to Amanda.

Then they are gone—over the side of the boat. Two splashes, a churning of water, the sound of swimmers' strokes, then the vacuum of darkness, lake, and night. If there's going to be a moon, it isn't up yet.

"One of them should have stayed with us," Amanda whispers.

"But they can't ever be apart," Francie says. "They can't stand to be separated."

✻

The night has many parts to it. Time elongates like an accordion, giving off atonal, madness-making music. Waiting is both flat and endless and so intensely concentrated that it exhausts them. The girls lean against each other, breathing hard. At one point the boat rocks sharply.

"What's that! Do they have whales here?" Amanda gasps.

"No, it's the Peachtree Loch Ness Monster."

They both begin to laugh, like maniacs, like lunatics, choking until they cry.

"How long, do you think, before a person will freeze to death?" Amanda asks finally.

"In Georgia, in springtime, it probably takes a week."

Again they shake the boat with their laughter.

Then they are quiet. They wait, hearing night birds cry from the trees.

"My God," Amanda says. "Liz is cooking a roast. Bill is waiting at the Greyhound Station."

"That's in the other world," Francie says. "We're in this one, now. We can't worry about that."

"I knew I should have stayed home and studied for finals."

"This is like a final," Francie says. "If we can pass this one, we can pass anything."

# 23

# The Other World

When finally Francie and Amanda hear the buzz of a motor coming across the lake, they have passed through several zones of existence. They have slept briefly, stretching out on the floor of the boat, their legs woven under or over the center seat, like reeds of a grass mat. They have passed from chilled to frozen to numb and back to merely cold.

Both girls have peed into the tin can, having forgiven each other for the necessity. They have promised each other that in the morning, if they are still unrescued, they will swim to the populated shore and be saved. They have talked about secrets they had not dreamed of discussing in all the weeks they lived together in the house. (The Mystery of the Twins has been the great conundrum of their lives.) In these hours out of time they have come to love and depend on the sound of each other's voices.

When it's clear from the approaching roar that the cave of their intimacy will now be invaded, they bolt upright on the seat, they hug each other good-bye. They wait to be transformed into the girls they were— creatures from that other dimension.

Francie's earlier thought—How will they find us when they come back?—has now changed to—How will I live after this night? For she feels she's become another person. She's lived twenty-one years of having nothing (it seems) happen to her, and in the past months she has fallen into what she imagines as (she says the words to herself) "the churning cauldron of life."

As the grating motor noise gets closer, they see a light flash on and come toward them over the water— bright as a beacon, blinding.

"Francie! Amanda!"

The twins are yelling through some kind of bullhorn. The motor of their boat has cut off, and they're calling over the black water. "Can you hear us? Yell! Yell so we can find you."

Francie and Amanda yell. They scream. They bang the tin can on the side of the boat. They stamp their feet. The beam of light dances crazily over the water, missing them, bouncing about like a pinball. When finally they are located in the flood of brilliance, all is suddenly noise—the motor starting up again, the flailing of their little boat on the sudden waves, the icy slapping of the water over the sides and onto their bare legs.

Pandemonium—around them is shaking and vibration, shouts and instructions. The twins are bringing the larger motor boat alongside the smaller boat. One of the twins jumps into their boat and lands on Francie's feet. He lifts her up and hands her, bodily, over the dark wedge of water into the arms of the other twin. For a moment each man holds her sweetly, like a baby, close to his body. Then she is set down, left on her own.

Oh—the comfort and heat of a man's beating heart and solid chest. Till this instant, she has not thought of Joshua. But now her longing is so palpable, so intensely physical, that she feels her body will crumble if she is not held closely again, at once. The certainty overcomes her again—that she is not just herself but the instrument of some natural force that requires her to give herself up, to relinquish herself for the imperative of the species.

She *will* surrender! She has no choice. She will be forced to enter the flow of life despite herself. But she knows something new—choice is possible. She will not be incautious. She will not sacrifice herself. She knows that after nature is done with her, she will have to live with the consequences.

✳

The twins are talking their own language. Once both girls are in the larger boat, wrapped in rough blankets, the twins do things between themselves, between the two boats, with gas cans and oil cans and wrenches and rags and screwdrivers. In the light of the flashlight they keep exchanging between them, Francie sees they are each dressed in huge baggy overalls and flannel shirts.

After a time, the arrangements and conspiracies cease; the men separate into the two vessels and both motors begin to roar. They are moving now, back into time, into their futures, into that other world in which things go forward and happen and change and signify. Francie, longing for Joshua, desires to join that heated, beating world again, but not without a pang of regret for having to surrender that other, peaceful, frozen place.

✳

The twins are worried that Bill is waiting for them at the Greyhound Station. They are doubly worried that Liz is waiting for them at the cottage. All the newly-weds' glorious and romantic plans are messed up because two boys wanted to test out a motor. The twins mumble this concern to each other. They discuss this on dry land as their feet pound along the dark country road from Bailey's dock, each twin pulling one girl along by the hand. The boats are back in their places. Bailey may never know his was used; he may not even miss his overalls and shirts till next winter. It's not important; he won't care that they took his boat, rummaged in his house; he's like their father. He's known the twins since they were little kids.

Francie and Amanda don't talk at all; they need every bit of breath for running. The danger is over now that they are back in civilization. All Francie can think about is food and sleep.

But the twins still desire celebration. Getting Bill at the bus station is going to be a blast. Sure, he'll be mad as hell, but there's still the rest of the weekend. And Liz, her poor roast, it's probably a ball of cinders by now. She may be furious. She may be scared. She may have called out the sheriff. But it was one of those things. Out of gasoline. Dumb luck. But nothing serious. They still have the whole weekend before them.

✳

Amanda walks up the porch steps, opens the front door of the cottage, and screams.

"My God! Oh, my God! Liz is dead!"

They all crowd in the door and see Liz lying face down on the living room floor.

"She killed herself," Amanda cries.

"Get the windows!" a twin roars hoarsely. His monkey arms are throwing open window after window. "Carry her outside! It's the gas!"

A whiff of gas fills Francie's head, strong and bitter. Amanda is frozen in the doorway.

"Go outside!" a twin instructs her. "Both of you— *get outside*."

The twins have laid Liz down on the porch, they are fanning her face, talking to her, shaking her, begging her to wake up.

"She killed herself," Amanda sobs. "I know it. She's been depressed."

"No! She didn't!" The twin looks up from where he is poised over Liz's body. "She just didn't know you have to light the oven with a match. She must have just turned it on, and the gas filled up the house."

"Maybe she wanted to die. How can you be sure?" Amanda looks at Francie and says, "Even *you* told the army she was suicidal. She's been so miserable without Bill. Maybe she wanted to die and get it over with."

"Hey, listen—she just got married," one of the twins says. "She's a bride!"

"Is there a hospital in town?" Francie demands. "We have to get her there."

"Yeah," a twin agrees. "Get in the car!"

They run to the car, the two men carrying the unconscious bride, the others rushing behind. Francie looks back over her shoulder, half expecting to see the house blow up in a blast of broken stars.

✳

But before they have gone two miles, Liz begins to stir in the front seat. She flings an arm up and hits a twin on the side of the head. She yawns deeply. The cold air streaming in the windows has revived her. She looks around, baffled but alert. She smiles sweetly at Francie and Amanda in the back seat.

"We're taking you to the hospital," Amanda says. "We found you in the house, unconscious."

"Oh, no," Liz says. "I was just napping. I feel much better now."

"Did you want to die?"

"God, no. I was just making a salad and I felt sleepy."

She tells them she has no memory of time passing. She stretched out on the living room couch for a few minutes. That's all. She doesn't remember falling to the floor, doesn't know that Francie and Amanda were stranded for hours on the dark lake.

"I feel perfect," she says.

"Maybe we should still go and get you checked," Amanda says. "Maybe you have brain damage."

"They'd never be able to tell," Liz laughs. "No, I don't need the hospital! I need my husband. Won't he be waiting for me? Please, let's just go to the bus station. My soldier is waiting for me."

# 24

# The Hazel Wood

There must be an end to this night, but Francie can't imagine it will be in her lifetime. They enter the grimy Greyhound bus station to find Bill sleeping on a bench, his head on his duffel bag, his face pressed out of shape. On another bench, an old man is also sleeping, his face half-covered with newspapers. A ticket seller sits at the one open window staring dully out at the room, smoking a cigarette.

Bill looks waxen. His head is shaved. He is wearing a dark khaki uniform. When the twins wake him with war whoops and a couple of smacks on the back, he sits up, opens his eyes, and looks at them as if he's been tortured by the enemy and has no reserves of strength. Without his head of curls, he appears emaciated, weakened, almost helpless. At this hour of the night, in this

strange place, his gaze is disoriented and dull, the opposite of his usual shrewd, sharp glance. He stares at
them as if his brain has been scooped out.

Liz, letting out a small cry, goes to him and em-
braces him. She holds his face in her hands. As they fall
against each other, the twins turn their backs, walk
away, and pretend to study some posters of "Most
Wanted Criminals."

Francie can't take her eyes off the lovers—they are
whispering into each other's mouths, they are forehead
to forehead, they have forgotten that anyone else in the
world is alive.

This night, so bizarre, so wicked, and yet so innocent, a night during which they have toyed with natural
forces and tempted nature in an absurd and dangerous
way, has promised—till now—revelations and resolu-
tions. Now the fairy tale is winding down, and Francie
realizes she is not even in the story. She has become
irrelevant. And not only herself, but the twins and
Amanda, too. It would not distress the lovers at all (in
fact might please them) if the four of them suddenly
vaporized into thin air. She looks around to see if the
others are feeling this. The twins keep their eyes focused
on the photographs of criminals; Amanda is staring at
the candy machine, looking at the packets of stale crack-
ers and chewing gum.

It seems to Francie that they have all realized at the
same moment that they are expendable. The "gang" of
them—old buddies, housemates, college kids on a wild

weekend—has been reduced to extras on this stage wherein real life is taking place.

Francie glances back at the bench where Liz is crying and Bill is holding her loosely in his arms in a kind of passive defeat. They know they will have to part again in just a few hours.

Francie sways with faintness. She has gone beyond fatigue and hunger, beyond a kind of cosmic exhaustion. Now she feels she may fall down. She walks toward one of the twins, stands behind him, and presses her forehead into the ridge of his spine. He half twists around and puts his arm around her as she leans against him.

"Hey, girl," he says. "Hey, what's happening? Come on." He takes one look at her face, then picks her up and carries her outside to the car. He sets her gently in the back seat and climbs in after her. Then he holds her against him, rubbing her back, trying to stop her from shivering.

"I'm so cold," she explains. "I've never been this cold." As she begins to warm and quiet herself, she whispers to him, "Thank you. I really need to hold onto you for a minute or two."

"I'm good with that," he says. "Hold on as long as you want."

✳

Bill drives the car back to the cottage, drives fast with an arm around Liz, with the window open so that ice-cold air streams in over them all. A twin sits up front with them, giving Bill directions as the car flies along the dark country road. The twin talks in a low voice, giving short, exact commands—"Take a right at that row of mailboxes, bear left at the fork in the road." Francie sees a shiver run through him, hears his voice quake with chill. Amanda leans forward from the back seat and puts her hand on his neck. "Could you close that window, do you think?" she whispers to him. She strokes his neck a bit, seeming to want to warm him in the same way Francie's twin has been warming and comforting her. They owe something to these boys who swam across a lake to save their lives. How could they do less for them? So, in the freezing, flowing night, Amanda leans toward her twin and Francie leans into hers.

For it is fact, finally, though she still does not know which boy is which, she knows that, for tonight, one of them is hers.

✳

No one speaks when they reach the cottage. Zombie-like, they stumble up the path, into the house, in and out of the bathroom in their turn, then into the places they will sleep. Liz and Bill close the bedroom door and are gone. Francie notes that Amanda follows her twin to the living room, where she and he fall down on one of the couches. Her twin comes into the bedroom she and Amanda were to have shared and together they fall into one of the twin beds. He inches against her to hold and to warm her. She backs against his warmth and immediately falls asleep.

✴

Sometime during the early morning hours, there is a fierce, violent thunderstorm. The house bursts white with flashes of lightning; the sky sizzles. Boom after boom rocks the universe. Briefly, unafraid, Francie opens an eye, feels the heavy arm of the twin over her back, begins to fall into unconsciousness again. They move closer to each other like creatures in a cave, innocents in the Garden of Eden, huddled close for warmth and protection.

✴

When they awake, it is nearly noon. The women gather in the kitchen and cook. They all eat enormous portions of bacon and eggs, grits and potatoes. Some color has come into Bill's face, but Liz is alabaster-pale. Somehow it's decided that the twins will take Francie and Amanda into town, to the one movie theater there, and watch the double feature, two movies with Fred Astaire and Ginger Rogers. They do this, half-sleeping through both movies, and when that's over, they go to the Dairy Queen for hamburgers and milkshakes, and when they're finished with that, they wander through Woolworth's, looking at counters full of threads and aprons and lipsticks and underwear. Finally, they sit in a bar called One-Horse Shay, and they all drink beers. Francie thinks of Harvey Rubin, how he first bought her a beer and then led her into the world where Joshua could be discovered. *Joshua.* The thought of him almost undoes her! What has she done to him by being here, by abandoning him? Where is her conscience? She meant to hurt him, but what does that say about her?

✳

When the boys decide they have stayed away long enough, that it is acceptable for the four of them to make an appearance again, Francie's twin drives slowly, almost dreamily, back to the cottage on the dirt road. When they arrive, the twin—whom she now considers her own—follows her up the path saying, lovingly, without a shade of ridicule, "Hey, Francie, watch out, don't step on the stinging nehuls." From the house they hear threads of music coming to them on the wind. Liz is playing her guitar and singing:

> *I went out to the hazel wood,*
> *Because a fire was in my head,*
> *And cut and peeled a hazel wand,*
> *And hooked a berry to a thread;*
> *And when white moths were on the wing,*
> *And moth-like stars were flickering out,*
> *I dropped the berry in a stream*
> *And caught a little silver trout.*

# 25

# Cross Creek

Though Francie feels she's been away an eon, an eternity, she arrives back on campus and the weekend is not yet over. The remainder of Sunday night lies ahead—it's only early evening. Bill is already on the bus heading back to the army base. She and the others are back in Gainesville and in the house where they live together. After Francie unpacks her few things, she realizes she does not want to stay a minute longer in the house. She's had enough of all of them. She needs to think, to calm herself, to try to understand what has transpired this weekend.

She walks to the student union, thinking of something simple and comforting: coffee and a glazed doughnut. Normality is what she craves—automatic actions, automatic thoughts.

Just as she holds her thick white cup under the coffee spigot, Harvey Rubin appears behind her in line and says, "Let me pay for that, Francie. Then you'll owe me, and you'll have to be nice to me."

"I'm always nice to you," she says. She's really glad to see him, to hear a voice of sanity and familiarity.

"Where's your lover boy?" he asks.

"I haven't seen him this weekend," Francie says.

"I've had a punk weekend, too," he says. "Studying. Want to take a ride with me?"

"Where to?" She's thinking she's had enough riding this weekend.

"I could show you something very surprising," he says. "A secret place. . . ."

"Never mind."

"A literary experience."

"Meaning?"

"A famous writer used to live near Gainesville, Francie . . . out by Lochloosa Lake. At Cross Creek."

"Marjorie Kinnan Rawlings. I know she used to live there."

"Right—but you've never been to her house, have you? Want to go and see it tonight?"

Another proposition. Has she the energy?

"She was very smart, a cracker, but smart," Harvey says. "Did you know she willed her estate to the University of Florida? She'd turn over in her grave if she knew what was going on in her house now."

"What do you mean? What's going on?"

"You'll find out if you come there with me. We can be back in an hour. Maybe we'll even see a deer in the woods. You know that Marjorie Kinnan Rawlings won the Pulitzer prize for her book about a boy and a deer?"

"I know—I saw *The Yearling,* with Gregory Peck," Francie says. "About the boy who loved his deer so much. And then . . . look what happened. . . ."

"Pure *schmaltz,*" Harvey says. "Just so much tear-jerking."

"You're a bad man," Francie says.

"Then you should marry me, Francie. I've been reading about Rawlings. She wrote: *'A woman has got to love a bad man once or twice in her life, to be thankful for a good one.'*"

✳

They drive through the woods in Harvey's old car. The wind is soothing, full of the scent of bark and spring-time blooms. Francie is so tired that she feels like an organism about to expire—an amoeba under a microscope who has run out of protoplasmic fluid.

They turn up an old dirt road, and Francie's insides thump as the wheels of the car jerk over holes and fallen branches. The headlights of Harvey's car illuminate an engraved wooden sign at the entrance to the property. He stops the car for Francie to read it:

*It is necessary to leave the impersonal highway, to step inside the rusty gate and close it behind. One is now inside the orange grove, out of one world and in the mysterious*

*heart of another. And after long years of spiritual homeless-*
*ness, of nostalgia, here is that mystic loveliness of childhood*
*again. Here is home.—Marjorie Kinnan Rawlings, Cross*
*Creek, 1942*

"I'll tell you something, Francie—what's going on in her house is certainly the mysterious heart of another world, but not one she ever would have dreamed of."

He continues bumping along the road till they come in view of the flat one-story country house. Every window is alight. Music is bursting from the house—Francie hears the sound of men laughing.

"Come with me." Harvey gets out of the car and opens her door—her feet sink into the soft earth. Immediately there is the sound of a mosquito buzzing against her cheek. She slaps it away. Harvey takes her hand and leads her toward the house.

"The mysterious heart of a world," Harvey says. "Look inside."

Through the glass windows, Francie sees men dancing with each other. Two men are embracing on a couch. She hears a rustling close by and sees two men kissing on the verandah of the house.

"The Heart of Darkness," Harvey whispers to her. "Crime, but no Punishment."

She doesn't reply to him, but together they stand and watch the spectacle, the inversion of every love song she knows, of every movie she's seen—the contradiction of the universe: men in love with each other.

She's never really imagined it fully, guessed at its nature, but here it is, vivid, intense, and overwhelming.

"Have enough?" Harvey asks, after a few moments.

"How did you find out about this?"

"Dr. Winston, my French poetry teacher, made a pass at me, Francie. I mean, not so you'd know it exactly, but he invited me to a party out here; he said lots of artistic people liked to get together out in the woods, and was I interested? I figured out what he was asking me. I must look artistic, Francie—or too pretty for my own good . . . that's probably why he took a chance."

Francie can hardly talk. She is certain she sees her teacher, Professor Raskolnikov—his wavy hair, the curve of his shoulder—as he dances with a young man. Is it Emil? She can't be sure; his face is turned away from her.

"Could we go back now?"

Harvey puts his hand on her shoulder as they stand, looking into the house. "I had to see for myself," Harvey says finally. "You know, the English department is in charge of Cross Creek now—but I don't think anyone in it knows this is what it's being used for. Only a few professors know—the homosexuals—who discovered it and realized it could be a safe meeting place. Some of these teachers are married and have families, Francie. Amazing, isn't it? The varieties of human experience—you'd never guess how far it can go."

Francie isn't surprised just now at the extremities of human desire—she's seen enough of it lately to know that desire doesn't live meekly in a cage till summoned out.

*Nature, blind—has set us all ticking,* she thinks. *We are all nature's puppets.* Francie's skin is crawling. She slaps at herself, recoiling from the swarms of mosquitoes. The insects are buzzing around her eyes, brushing her forehead, threatening her soul. "Please, let's go!"

Harvey begins to lead her back to the car. A glint of moonlight suddenly outlines the shape of another car, hidden deep in the woods. Francie thinks she sees men in it. She nudges Harvey. "Look."

"Don't worry, he says. "It's probably a couple of lovers. That, or the FBI."

# 26

# Purge

On Monday morning, Francie sits in her Russian literature class, trying out her new Parker pen. The price tag (cost: $3.85) still hangs from the clip. Francie, dizzy with a sudden headache, is writing idly in her notebook, writing whatever comes to mind, waiting for class to begin. Professor Raskolnikov is late, which is odd. He is never late to class. He is always there early, often carrying his coffee cup and doughnut, bouncing about on his crepe-soled shoes, writing clever things on the blackboard.

Liz is not in class today; the weekend at Peachtree Lake exhausted her. She is still at the house, sleeping. Amanda is here in class, but she and Francie came separately. She is sitting far across the room, reading her Turgenev novel.

Francie checks the flow of her pen, which she has filled this morning with honey-brown ink—the color she always uses in her fountain pens. Now she shakes a few drops of ink on the page. She writes, randomly, without plan or logic:

*I am tired of breasts and curves*
*And poses and scents and colorful cheeks.*
*I want to sit on a gray rug in a gray shirt*
*With a pale face and be a woman without*
*Two pointed breasts to vouch for it.*
*I want to be calm and smell of myself*
*And know who I am, not stretch and twist and*
*Thrust to reassure myself I am headed in*
*The "right direction."*

Is that a poem? A pronouncement? Francie's mind is not clear; there's a feeling in her tongue as if it's grown larger than her mouth, as if it's dry and shaped like an enormous acorn. She idly writes:

*St. Louis Woman had a yen for men*
*She went to bed with a fountain pen*
*One night the pen broke and the ink went wild,*
*St. Louis Woman had a blue-black child.*

Francie wonders if she could be losing her mind. She recalls a feverish dream she had last night after Harvey delivered her back to her house. She writes it down now, with her honey-brown ink:

*I am on the dark back porch of our house in Brooklyn.*
*My parents are with me in the darkness watching shoot-*
*ing stars. Suddenly a great flashing flare of light, a ball of*
*fire, is descending upon us. We all scream in fear. I see the*

*terror in my parents' eyes. They want to save me, but they can't. The fireball falls into our midst, a flaming spear, and then all is quiet. No one seems hurt. My father shows us that he has caught the shooting star in his bare hands. It is black and charred, small, ashen, and pock-marked, like a small basketball with holes in it. He offers it to me, a dead thing, and I refuse it. I want a burning, beautiful star.*

"I want a star," Francie writes in her notebook. "Nothing less."

Her professor is more than a half hour late. A few classmates are packing up and leaving. Others are talking to one another. Francie now feels a tight band circling her head. There are lights flashing behind her eyes, shooting stars she can almost catch with her eyelashes, wild stars shooting in her inner firmament.

Someone enters the classroom, a man Francie does not recognize, and brandishes a piece of chalk. He writes on the blackboard, in huge scrawling letters:

NO CLASS TODAY. YOUR PROFESSOR WILL BE UNABLE TO TEACH THIS CLASS FOR THE REMAINDER OF THE TERM. A SUBSTITUTE TEACHER WILL BE ASSIGNED BY THE NEXT CLASS MEETING.

A buzz goes up among the students—everyone accosts the man, asking, "What's wrong? Where is he? What happened to our professor? Why won't he be back?"—but the man, who is wearing a black suit and a black tie, just holds up his hands to ward off questions and says, "Sorry, sorry. I'm just bringing the message."

Francie closes her notebook, sweeps her books on top of it, and stands to leave class. Her knees buckle; she almost falls.

She looks toward Amanda, who is already hurrying out of class. Francie tries to call her name, but now her voice feels choked off. She can't even speak. She staggers out the door of Anderson Hall and heads toward a bench just off the path.

"Francie!"

She lifts her head to see Emil, the French boy, coming toward her. The light in the sky is far too bright; she covers her eyes with her hands.

"There's no class," she says with her eyes closed as she feels Emil sit beside her. "My professor, your Leon—well, he wasn't there today," Francie says. "Class was canceled. Someone told us he won't be back."

"Leon is gone," Emil says. The sound of his voice makes Francie opens her eyes. Emil is wild-eyed; his blond curls are shaking with agitation. "They came to the house this morning to accuse him. They told him not to deny anything because they have proof, they have statements from others, they have photographs of us. They went to all the other professors they could find. They're gone, too, Francie. Fired. Kaput. Packed up and run off. Ruined. Some of them have wives and kids. Everything is ruined—whole lives gone up in smoke."

"What do you mean?"

"I shouldn't sit here with you too long," Emil says. "If their spies see me talking to you, they may question you. And, if they do, remember, don't get involved. You don't know anything about us."

"What do I know?" she asks, totally puzzled.

"You know what you know," Emil says. "You were at our house. You met us at the opera."

"Oh, but what does that prove?" She does not say she thinks that she saw them dancing together in the house in the woods last night.

"Oh, Francie, sweetheart. They've done a witch-hunt. They couldn't find communists, so they picked opera lovers, Francie. Art lovers. They fired so many. Not just Leon, but Chargill, who does Shakespeare, and Winston, who does French poetry, and Froscher, who does Dryden and Pope, and Wessler, who teaches voice, and Plimpton in theater arts—and McGee, who is the organist. They've been following us for months, spying, asking questions, looking in our windows." Emil puts his head in his hands. "There's a place we all sometimes gather out in the country—and I think they've found out about that, too. I don't know yet if they'll kick me out of school—I'm only a student. They might think I was coerced."

"I don't understand this," Francie says. "This is America." Red, white, and blue wheels spin behind her eyes. She stands up and just as suddenly has to lie down in the grass at the side of the bench. "Excuse me, Emil," she says politely and gives in to an overwhelming need to put her body on the ground, and her face against the cool grass.

Emil kneels beside her. "Francie, what's wrong?"

"Something bad is happening to me, Emil."

"Do you have that terrible flu germ, do you think?"

"I was on a lake with ducks," she says. "The smell. . . ."

Emil touches her forehead. "Francie, you're burning with fever. I read about this in the student paper. You must have the Asian flu. The epidemic is hitting all over campus. You're probably coming down with it. Let me help you walk home."

"I can't move," she says. She begins to cry. Then she vomits. A black curtain descends over her head; she gives in to the darkness.

✳︎

The halls of the infirmary are filled with beds, and the beds are filled with students. Francie is led by a nurse to one of the beds and made to lie down wearing all her clothes. "You'll have an ice bag or an aspirin, whichever I find first," she explains to Francie. "We're running out of everything. I don't even have a thermometer to use to take your temperature. But it's high," she assures Francie. "So I'll try to find you an ice bag."

All around her people are groaning or sobbing or throwing up—she sees a boy in the bed opposite hers; he's still as a corpse, he's staring at the ceiling. He doesn't even blink. Emil has disappeared. No one else knows where she is. When she doesn't come back to the house, will Liz call her parents and report that she is missing?

Will she ever see anyone again that she knows? It doesn't matter. She is on fire. She is burning into a dark cinder. She imagines herself lying on a bed of ice cubes. She yearns for a single ice cube, a cloudy frozen cube bigger than a mountain. Now she is sliding down one of these icy mountain slopes with her bare thighs touching the glassy surface. Her skin fuses to the ice as she skids downhill. She is skinned as she flies, so that when she reaches the bottom of the mountain she is wearing only a garment of gleaming arteries and veins. Blue and green blood vessels, glowing with neon brilliance, are her jewels, her beautiful, gleaming decorations.

✼

Now she has been wheeled into the gymnasium, under a basketball hoop. Hundreds of cots surround her, and on each one is a writhing figure. A symphony of coughing rises to the rafters, coughing in every key, in every rhythm, loud, endless whooping coughs; deep, phlegmy, choking coughs; high, dry, barking coughs. Francie has no voice at all. She has not eaten for days, only taken sips of water or juice, or nothing at all when her cup is empty and no one comes to check on her.

She is outside of time once again, in that place where nothing is real. There is no connection to history. The future may be safely dismissed for the moment; even the present moment demands no services to be performed, offers no instructions, asks for no observance of responsibility.

Francie sleeps, Francie coughs, Francie now and then staggers on a nurse's arm to a bathroom, where she is held up as she lowers herself to the seat, relieves herself, and is led back. The fever is relentless, her body racked by chills, soaked by sweat; the aching in her limbs becomes an entertainment. How long can she bear it before she cries out, waves a limp arm, begs for a nurse, an ice bag, an aspirin?

The nurses are rationing aspirins; only if the fever is so high, only if the pain is so severe, only if you show signs of delirium. Only if your parents appear at your bedside and demand that you get a pill or they will sue the university.

Francie suspects she may never see her parents again. It doesn't matter—one day they will all fly on angels' wings and meet in heaven. She is surprised at this thought but remembers that her mother told her this one day in her childhood. She knows that her mother believes that dead is dead. She knows her mother is completely skeptical about such things as heaven and flying there on angels' wings. Why would she have told her that? But how nice that she did. How lovely an idea it is, all that flying through the pearly blue air with a cool wind blowing one's hair. All those soft, white, cottony clouds to perch upon. Heaven is the ultimate comfort, whereas here on earth, in the gymnasium, all is pain, noise, discomfort, heat, and ultimate loneliness.

No one can visit her. No one can see her. She is contaminated. She is contagious, dangerous, poisonous. She is dying. How unexpected this death is—but how convenient. For now all those decisions about the future are wholly academic. The university and its plague have made her future academic. This is appropriate.

Someone is impatiently spooning some hot farina into her mouth. "You need to keep your strength up," the person says. "At least drink." Then the person is gone. The contents of the bowl, resting on her sheet, congeals into warm cement, then turn cold and heavy as lead. She taps the bowl with her spoon and hears a heavenly chord.

She begins to sing a song her mother used to play on the piano:

*Seated one day at the organ, I was weary and ill at ease,*
*And my fingers wandered idly over the noisy keys.*
*I knew not what I was playing or what I was dreaming then—*
*But I heard a chord of music like the sound of a great*
    AMEN.
LIKE THE SOUND OF A GREAT AMEN.

When Francie stops singing, Joshua's face looms above her. He has a wide smile, a Cheshire cat smile, on his exquisite, magnificent, enormous face. His face could be a basketball in the hoop above her, coming down, lowering itself to cover her face and smother her.

She coughs right at him, but his vast face won't be dislodged. All he says, over and over again, is "Francie,

Francie, Francie. Where were you? I looked for you all weekend. I came to your house every day. Why did you leave me?"

"Get away. I'm floating up now. You can't be here. You'll catch this terrible plague."

"So I'll catch it," he says. And he stays. He sits, immovable, heavy as a tank, on her cot. He won't be pushed away when she kicks him. He washes her face with a wet cloth; he makes her sip water; he tries to feed her the congealed cement. He runs his hand gently over the sheet that covers her legs, but her skin is still flayed from the slide down the ice mountain. Or missing entirely. His touch burns and scrapes her; she forces his hand away.

"I don't want to get married," she says.

"You don't have to."

"I don't want to be a school teacher," she says.

"You don't have to."

"I don't want to have a baby."

"You don't have to do anything you don't want to do, Francie."

"I don't want to die."

"You won't die. I'll stay here and see to it."

"Good," Francie says. "You see to it."

# 27

# Phi Beta Kappa

*D*ear Mom and Dad:

 *I have lots of news to tell you, so here goes:*

 *1. You may have heard of the awful Asian flu epidemic that swept the campus; well, now I can tell you that I had it, too! (That's why you haven't had a letter from me in a while.) But I'm getting much better, though I lost twelve pounds and was in the infirmary for ten days. I'm a little worn out now, but I am going back there three times a week for B-12 shots, which the doctor thinks will increase my appetite and help build up my resistance. You don't need to worry about me or call long-distance, since I am getting back to normal and preparing for the end of the term . . . and for GRADUATION!*

 *2. Which brings me to tell you some good news: I have been tapped to Phi Beta Kappa! Can you believe it? There will be a ceremony and dinner next Friday night, and then I will get my little gold key! I hope you are proud of me—the first person in our family to graduate from college—and what's more, "with high honors"! I will soon be writing you details about exactly when and where commencement exercises will take place and will find out motel rates so that you can make reservations for that weekend.*

*3. I know you are concerned about my future plans, so let me tell you what I have been thinking about. I may go on to graduate school! I have an appointment with the Dean next week to discuss my qualifications for a graduate fellowship in the English department. I know you both had hoped I would decide to become an elementary school teacher, but I know for sure this is not what I want to do. Neither is there a wedding in store for me in the near future. (Though I do care a great deal for that young man I wrote you about before. Joshua and I are good friends, and you will probably be able to meet him at graduation. But he and I have a long way to go before we can discuss anything like a permanent arrangement.)*

*4. I have some other ideas for what I might do. The most exciting is that I am applying to* Mademoiselle *to go to New York, and—if I win the contest—I could work for the summer on the staff of the magazine! Read this article I'm gluing onto this letter. It will give you an idea of what got me started thinking in this direction. Here it is:*

Miss Louisa Hay of *Mademoiselle*'s College and Career

Department will be on campus this week to meet and talk to undergraduates about the magazine's College Board Contest. Girls interested in writing, art, fashion design, and publishing can arrange to meet her through the Office of the Dean of Women. The contest offers an opportunity for girls to come to New York for a salaried month in June to work on *Mademoiselle*'s August college issue.

During her visit, Miss Hays will talk to English and art professors and to undergraduates about *Mademoiselle*'s current fiction and art contests.

*So—can you just see me in New York, dressed in heels and a fancy suit, among all those skyscrapers? Of course, I am a New Yorker by birth. But you know I have always been interested in writing, and this would be such a great opportunity if I were chosen! (Did I ever tell you that Thomas Wolfe, a great writer who also lived in Brooklyn, died the same year I was born? I sometimes think it is my fate to fill his shoes.) By the way, girls who win guest editorships at* Mademoiselle *sometimes go on to get very good jobs in New York. Some are offered editorial jobs. Others become writers! You know I have always loved to read—and write, too. Who knows what might happen? I wrote a poem while I was getting the flu—I was probably delirious when I wrote it!—and sent it to* Seventeen *magazine. If they accept it, they might even pay me! So*

✳ _____

*keep your fingers crossed for me . . . and in case I haven't
told you this before, I want to thank you both for all the
sacrifices you've made so I could go to college, and for all
the love you have given me.*

*Your grateful child,*
*Francie*

# 28

# "You Women Have a Habit . . ."

In the dean's mahogany-paneled office, before his huge carved desk, Francie sits dressed in a gray and blue wool suit, blue high-heeled shoes, white gloves, a small felt hat, and, underneath it all, a girdle! (She has Mary Ella Root to thank for her manners and appearance; she has even curled her eyelashes this day.)

The dean of students, Dr. Guy Franklin, a small man with a tight mouth, sits at his desk reading Francie's transcript. On it are all the courses she has taken during the past four years, all her grades, her honors, her placement test results, her grade-point average for each term. She knows her record is impeccable. She sits there, ready to smile and accept congratulations, ready to say yes, indeed, she will be pleased to accept a fellowship to graduate school, she will do the university proud.

She can feel herself, at this moment, at the cusp of freedom; all her life she has been in a long tunnel, and finally she is about to burst into clear air and open skies.

Around her neck, on a delicate fourteen-karat-gold chain, she is wearing her Phi Beta Kappa key, presented to her by the president of the university chapter at the formal dinner held the week before in the student union. She and six chosen students (the others all men, with their girlfriends beaming beside them) sat at the table of honor while praises were heaped upon them.

Beside Francie sat Joshua, handsome as a bride-groom in his dark suit. He squeezed her hand hard when her name was called to come up and receive her Phi Beta Kappa key.

Now, as she waits for the Dean to look up from her record file, she recalls seeing this morning, as she walked across campus to his office, a sign in some girl's window that read: "I'll say I DO by '62—or DIE!"

Has something in Francie finally blotted out that requirement to mate embossed in her very genetic material? Perhaps the Asian flu has altered the chemistry of her brain, changed her biological imperative, repro-grammed the pathways of her thinking. The fact is, there's something urgent in her that wants growing and learning. Just as Joshua has asserted his right to make his way in the world, she, too, has felt this expansion inside herself.

There have been external signals, too—her term paper about Anna Karenina, returned by the substitute teacher in her Russian lit class, had Professor Raskolnikov's comments on it: *"Francie, an A-plus paper. You have the goods. You can do anything, my dear. Keep this image sharp and clear before the minutiae. You must destroy all your old limitations now and do something you did not know was in you, or your luck may leave you."*

Where was he now, poor Professor Raskolnikov, he and all the other teachers who had been found out, revealed, unraveled? And her beautiful friend Emil—he, too, had vanished like a wraith into thin air after delivering her, that day of her collapse, to the infirmary from which she had fought her way into the light again.

Francie likes to think that somehow she has made a hero's journey, far into the nether world and back, as her literary heroes before her have done. But what injustices she has seen along the way, done to herself, to her friends! How unfairly they have been judged, and for reasons having no connection to their human selves.

Dr. Guy Franklin now looks up from the sheaf of papers he is examining, removes his eyeglasses, and looks at Francie through his small dark eyes.

"Well," he says. "You are a fine student."

"Thank you," says Francie.

"And I see here that you have excellent letters of recommendation, an admirable scholastic record, outstanding achievement scores."

"Thank you," Francie repeats.

"The problem is," he says, and Francie feels her heart skip, just under her Phi Beta Kappa key. "The problem is that you women have a habit of changing your minds about teaching, and instead you tend to run off and get married. Over the years, we have been burned many times. So I must say I'm sorry, my dear, that I can't offer you a graduate fellowship, or even an assistantship to teach a class to incoming freshman. These jobs are best offered to men. We've just had too many females run out on us at the last minute—they come in wearing a big smile and flashing an engagement ring, and they apologize that they've had a change of plans and they're so sorry. Then we're in trouble. We end up not having the proper number of teachers for our students, and we're in a major bind."

What can Francie possibly say to him? She stares at his face.

"It won't hurt you to work out in the world for a short time before some man snaps you up," Dr. Guy Franklin says. "You're an attractive girl, yes, not bad at all. I can promise you it won't be long before you have your 'MRS.'"

Francie observes his face melt and drip in blobs through her blaze of tears. She stands up, wobbling on her high heels, and walks out of his office.

In the hall, she tears off her white gloves, her little felt hat. Then, in the ladies' room, she tugs off her girdle and throws it into the trash. Finally, she washes her face, rubbing the curl from her eyelashes, the lipstick from her mouth. With the frills gone, she takes a good long look into her own fierce blue eyes. There is nothing blurry in what she sees before her. The scales have fallen from her eyes. She is energized, clear-minded, ready for the work that lies ahead. All that remains is to do it.

# 29

# New York, New York

*hat do you have to say . . . or draw . . . or promote . . . or design? What do you consider to be the hot issues or great causes of our times? Write an article taking a stand."* On Francie's desk are the rules of *Mademoiselle's* College Board Contest. *"Or write a sketch of a college, town, campus, hangout, department, organization, professor, student, or tradition. Comment on one of the following: formal dances, hazing, the honor system, social rules, unwritten laws or taboos.*

*For the twenty College Board Members who have done the best work, we offer a trip to New York, and a month with pay on the staff of* Mademoiselle *as a Guest Editor in June. You're eligible if you're a woman undergraduate at an accredited college, under twenty-six. Besides having a hand in* Mademoiselle's *college issue, you'll be shown New York—parties, the theater, manufacturing and publishing houses—and interview a celebrity of your choice. Send entries to: College Board Contest,* Mademoiselle, *575 Madison Avenue, New York 22."*

Francie has a lot to say about the "hot issues" of our time; she has already made notes for her essay about Professor Raskolnikov and his friend and lover, Emil. Of course, she will change their names. The "hot issue," the "great cause" she wants to address is the idea of personal freedom. Though she is not a homosexual male, she feels she has been deprived during her college years by curfews, restrictions, dress codes. Freedom has been denied her because of her sex, her *mere gender,* by the sinister idea of stereotyping, the concept that permitted the Dean just this morning to accuse her of being one of those "unreliable" women who might show up flashing an engagement ring at him. She knows she's not "one of them"—she's herself, Francie. She's reliable, unique, and one of a kind.

Oh, indeed, she has quite a lot to say. She flings the cover off her little black Smith-Corona portable, rolls in a sheet of paper, and begins typing. She stops once, after an hour, to go into the kitchen for a peanut butter and jelly sandwich. There she finds Amanda at the table, spinning a salt shaker, humming to herself, smiling a slightly mad smile.

"You look a bit strange," Francie remarks.

Amanda raises her hand and waves it at Francie.

"Why are you waving at me? Oh no, don't tell me. . . ." for, just as Mary Ella Root had done (just as the Dean fears all women will do), Amanda is flashing an engagement ring at her. A diamond sparkles on her left hand. Amanda's fair face is blushing rose-color.

"Who?" Francie says. "What happened? Who is he?"

"Jerry."

Jerry. At first the word makes no sense. Who is Jerry? Jerry who? Francie says it out loud. "Jerry who?"

*"Jerry who? What do you mean? Our Jerry!"*

A twin. Jerry. My God! Francie leans against the refrigerator. Amanda has named a twin. Which one could he be—and what about the other one? "When . . . why are you . . . ? How . . . ?" Francie can't form a sentence.

"It had to happen. We finally realized we were in love, Francie. You know how this magic time is all ending? Our living together this term, our being with one another? Jerry and I realized we really have to graduate, we have to go on and have our lives. So we had to make a decision—after all this, after our time at Peachtree Lake, after that night, after what happened during the lightning storm in the cottage . . . it was that storm, Francie."

"What happened during the storm, Amanda?"

Amanda casts her eyes down; her golden lashes rest on her blushing cheek.

"It just happened that night, Francie, when we slept together on the couch. We couldn't help it."

A great chasm opens in Francie's breast, some hole she didn't know was there. An icy wind blows through it, chilling her to the bone. Tears, for the second time that day, fill her soul, unbidden. How carefully she has guarded herself, when she could have known so much. She, too, was with a twin the night of that storm. Is she sorry she has nothing to confess?

Amanda takes Francie's tears for joy. She stands up and comes to hug her. "I know you're happy for me, Francie, and if anyone knows how wonderful the twins are, you know, don't you?"

"Oh, yes, I know," Francie says. "I know how wonderful the twins are. But . . ."

"But what?"

"How can you tell which one is which?" Francie begins to laugh, and Amanda joins in; they cling to each other, giggling with a wild, improbable hysteria.

"I can't always tell," Amanda confesses. "But I figure . . ." here they burst into laughter again . . . "I figure the one who wants me will know who I am!"

They hear a noise in the hall and quiet themselves. A twin comes walking into the kitchen and avoids looking at them. From his expression, his serious, downcast look, his distant, dour glance, Francie knows this is clearly not the bridegroom-to-be.

He, then, the twin who must be Bobby, says nothing but carefully keeps his eyes from the women, walks through the kitchen and out. Francie watches him recede down the hall, sees the little indentation on the delicate back of his neck, that small, bare, vulnerable place where she knows an arrow has pierced him. His loss illuminates him. She can't console him. His brother has betrayed him.

✳

In her room, she takes the clay penis from its hiding place and smashes it with both hands, hitting it on her desk top. She will not play games any longer; she will no longer toy with essential, primal matters in a precious, coy, ignorant manner. Now she will take matters into her own hands in every sense and direct her life accordingly. This is the moment to "hold the light" (as her father once admonished her mother), to direct its strong beam, and to see exactly what must be done.

Then she phones Joshua.

✳

They meet at the bench in the fading light of the spring evening. She precedes him under the canopy of leaves, holding back the branches so that he can pass beneath the low ones. He moves into their familiar cave like a strong dark animal, his body dense and muscular, his eyes holding and questioning hers.

She has loved him all the more since he ministered to her and risked his very life during the days of the plague epidemic. Each day he had come faithfully to the infirmary, to the makeshift hospital in the gymnasium, bringing her school books when she was able to read, bringing her special foods to tempt her, sitting at her side as she slept fitfully. During the days after her fever broke, he sat beside her cot, holding her hand, enduring the shower of germs from the other coughing students, reassuring and comforting her. Finally, on the day when she was given permission to be discharged, he helped her to stand up, supported her as she walked slowly outside, weak and shaking, and guided her into the taxi he had called to deliver her back to her house.

During and after her slow recovery, they had stopped their bench-life; he was too polite and considerate to suggest it, and she didn't long for it. She had no time, no energy for their sapping activities, for their dead-end love-making, for their futureless, cryptic conversations.

He comes under the tree now, looking hopeful, arms spread wide to embrace her, thinking perhaps her phone call was the signal that she is ready to receive him again. She hugs him warmly, she rubs her forehead deeply against the rounded knob of his shoulder, she wraps herself against his cave of his ribs, she strokes his back, caresses the ridges of his spine that curve like the bow of a great ark.

When she looks at his face, she sees his contented smile. Whatever this invitation is about, he is deeply pleased. His teeth are so beautiful, his mass of dark curls a bouquet, his broad jaw squared to cherish and protect her. She laughs with pleasure.

But *what*, his smile asks. *What*, his eyes ask her.

She says it straight; she tells him what she wants.

"I want to go away with you for a weekend," she tells him. "We have only this one weekend before graduation. Then our parents will be here, we'll be too busy to see each other—and then we will be gone, separated from each other. To the four corners of the earth. You to graduate school, and me—well, who knows? Maybe to New York. But the fact is, we're going to be separated."

"Whatever I have to do is for *us*, Francie. If I leave you, it's because I'm trying to plan for our future. So that ultimately so we can have our lives together."

She shakes her head, she does not want to hear this, that his going away is really all for her. She has no engagement ring to wave in anyone's face, nor does she want one.

"I have things I want to do, too, Joshua. But I've decided I don't want to postpone this part of my life any longer. Nor can I live it on a bench. So—I want you to get us a hotel room, and I want to go away for a night with you."

His face is deeply serious as he studies her. He strokes her cheek with the back of his hand. "Do you know what you're saying?'

"Yes."

"You're not worried?"

"Not about that. I already went through those worries," she says. "We can figure that part out safely."

"But even if we do this . . . I still have to go away to

grad school, Francie. I have years of schooling ahead of me."

"Joshua—I have plans, too. My point is, I want this now. We don't have to make promises, set dates. This is now, we're here, we love each other."

"Oh, yes, we do love each other," he agrees.

"So I want to be with you in the real sense."

"You know how much I would love to, Francie. You know how much I want you. If you're sure."

"I'm very sure."

"Then I'll figure it out. For this coming weekend?"

"Yes, that would be good," she says.

"And you know what it means? That there's no going backward if we do this?"

"It means we'll be going forward."

"Yes," he says, looking a little frightened.

"Definitely forward," Francie says. "Don't worry. I'm not going to worry. I'm very happy with this idea. Okay?"

"Okay," Joshusa says, holding onto her. "Okay. Definitely okay."

# 30

## Life!

Galvanized with new purpose, Francie does a thousand things in a day. She goes to the sports stadium to be fitted for her cap and gown, orders her invitations and tickets for graduation, turns in all her final homework assignments, completes her required term papers, studies for her last exams. She begins to pack up her room for departure.

When a letter comes from *Seventeen* magazine, Francie opens it with the same kind of efficiency and determination that makes up her new rhythm:

> *Dear Reader of* Seventeen:
> *Your poem, "I Am Tired of Breasts," has been selected for publication in our regular section "IT'S ALL YOURS."* *We are happy to accept your submission and enclose*

*herewith a check for $25. We ask that you send us some
biographical information about yourself. Congratulations!
(signed) The Editors of* Seventeen

Yes! Francie clasps the letter hard. Yes! She actually
expected good news, counted on it. This attitude is
part of her new master plan—to think of herself as if
she has power. She begins to make a mental list of what
she will need to take to New York with her when *Mademoiselle* chooses her as a winner in its College Board
Contest. She can taste her victory. It's going to happen.

✳

In the meantime, Joshua has assignments of his own,
which he reports to Francie that he has completed. He
has arranged to borrow a car for the weekend; he has
called ahead to reserve a room in the Blue Seagull
Hotel in Jacksonville. He's gone to Woolworth's to buy
a fake wedding band, and he has also (when he tells
Francie this, he lowers his voice) "gone to the drugstore." Francie knows this means he has bought a pack-
age of rubbers, objects generally hidden from the eyes
of women, the first and only one of which Francie ever
saw dangling from a light fixture in Broward Hall.

Indeed, she has set into motion a plan that gathers
weight and speed as it moves toward its execution. The
thing that remains for Francie to do is tell Liz and
Amanda that she will be gone for the weekend—and
why.

She chooses a moment when the twins are away—
which is nearly all the time now. The fact is that the
brothers have been sliced in two since the sudden,
astonishing appearance of the engagement ring on
Amanda's finger. They speak to no one, not to each
other, not to Francie, not, when in each other's company, to Amanda or to Liz. They hang about morosely
in separate rooms of the house, their shoulders
hunched, their eyes so often on the floor that Francie
learns to sidestep their advancing crew-cut heads when,
blindly, they approach her in the hallways.

Amanda's engagement ring has become the glitter-
ing, icy wedge of the brothers' exile from each other.

✳

"You can't mean it!" Amanda says when Francie tells
Amanda and Liz she's going away with Joshua for the
weekend. "I don't believe it! Aren't you afraid the hotel
clerk will ask if you're married? Won't you feel guilty?
Wouldn't you rather do it the right way?" She holds
up her hand, flashing her engagement ring. "Really,
Francie—if you're feeling that intensely about Joshua,
wouldn't you rather get engaged? Or married? It's so
much safer. I mean—think of it. If you got pregnant, it
would be an awful mess, wouldn't it?"

"I don't want to get married," Francie explains. "I
don't know if you can understand that, but I *really*
don't want to. I have things I need to do first. How
could I go to New York if I were married? How could I
do anything but start wearing an apron and raising

babies? When a *man* says he has things to do, no one argues with him."

"Of course not," Amanda says, as if Francie is extremely backward. "He has to do his things if he's going to support a family. Which is why, when Jerry and I get married, I'm going to work so Jerry can get his master's in engineering and then his Ph.D."

"That sounds as if *you'll* be supporting the family, doesn't it?"

"But it's not real. It's not forever."

"Why should you do anything that's not real, Amanda?" Francie asks her. "Aren't you just as real as Jerry? Isn't what you want to do as important as what he wants to do?"

"Like what? What would I want to do? I mean, if not this."

"That's the question we never ask ourselves," Francie says. "That's my point."

"You amaze me, Francie, you are so determined lately," Liz says. "Maybe I had an influence on you." She comes toward Francie and kisses her. "Congratulations, anyway, is what I say. You go right ahead and have this weekend and enjoy every minute of it. Being a virgin isn't good for a girl after a certain point, anyway. It gets in the way, grows to be a bigger subject than it deserves. Once you get your virginity out of the way, you can think about other things."

"Like what?" Amanda asks again.

Francie is waiting on the front porch with her little suitcase when, on Saturday morning, Joshua pulls up to the house driving a borrowed red MG convertible. The smile on his face is at the same time subdued, shy, and charged with a bold electricity. Liz rushes out and gives Francie one last hug. "Now," she whispers, "when you come back, Francie, we'll truly be sisters in passion."

Just then, loping along the tree-covered street, one of the twins comes into view, his arms filled with heavy books. Drafting and graph papers stick at all angles out of his notebooks. Francie, for once, knows which twin this is. He is her twin-of-the-lake, she feels it in her blood. It's in the look he gives her, a grief-stricken, hollow look of need that twists her breath, makes her swallow hard. The purpose of her departure is as evident, she thinks, as if she were running naked into the arms of Joshua at this moment.

She wishes she could embrace her twin, thank him, tell him she will never forget the night on the lake, the night in the cottage, the night with him during the storm. But she can only smile, waving shyly, as she steps down from the porch to meet Joshua, who now stands beside the car to hold open the door for her.

The twin pauses wordlessly. At a loss for words, Francie gestures at the car, inviting him to admire it. To her it is only a piece of tin on wheels, the flying machine that will take her to the top of the mountain. But Francie is relieved that he has this passion for machines. At least a machine is constant; it will be there for him when human beings fail him.

He and Joshua exchange glances; they say a few monosyllabic admiring words about the car, nod their approval of it, almost seem to forget that Francie is present. But finally Joshua puts a hand on Francie's shoulder and guides her inside the car, puts her little suitcase in the trunk. She and her twin exchange one last look. Joshua, who has kept private the passions of his past, will, in turn, never know about her idyll at the lake. Francie adjusts her skirt carefully on the seat, puts her handbag on the floorboard, and waves good-bye to her old life.

✻

So—here they are at last: in a hotel. In a room with a lock on the door, with curtains drawn shut over the windows, with a vast soft private bed to share. No bride and groom could be more tender toward each other, could cherish each other with more adoration, delight, solicitous attention. No exchange of vows could fill them with more awe than they are filled with now. He and she both cry a little, for their own bravery, for the danger they now face in having to separate after this moment, when all the days of existence will not be, cannot be, like this day.

✻

They have food sent up to their room. In the dreamy steam of the shower, they laugh as their faces cloud and disappear into mist, only to emerge fresh and shining new all over again.

237

All thoughts, all words, defer to sensation. When Joshua rises above her, it's as if an ocean wave hangs suspended, quivering, balancing, a wave of such enormity—about to fall but not yet able to fall, holding itself with exquisite tension until it can no longer be borne, until it comes crashing down upon her, and they are under it and they are both lost in the swirling and foaming whirlpool.

How many times they are reborn in this one night and two days! Francie loses count as they meet and part, laugh and cry, join and separate. She learns there is a way in this life to step out of time, to exist somewhere else, in another plane of existence. What a sly bargain nature has made with us, she thinks. How cunning, how deeply, cunningly generous.

✳

On the way back to campus, driving slowly in the fast racing car, they are full, in every way. There is not a word to say, not a song to sing. They are both (Francie knows) totally peaceful, joyful, restful. The top is down, and the wind is a balm to them. Joshua reaches across the stick shift for Francie's hand. He clasps it in his, and she glances over to see his beautiful, strong profile, his teeth shining in the sunlight as he smiles, then laughs out loud, a surprised, confident, astonished laugh of amazement.

Yes, she thinks. We are in this hallowed place. I am having my life at last.

# 31

# There's No Stopping
# Me Now

Francie waves Joshua away with a kiss, watches him drive off, and turns to walk into the house. She feels herself float over the threshold. Liz, her face ragged with concern, greets Francie from where she has sunk into an old chair in the living room.

"You won't believe this," Liz says.

"Something bad?"

"Something really bad."

"Someone . . . died?" Faces flash before her. Her mother, her father, Mary Ella, Professor Raskolnikov, Emil . . .

"Bobby ran off with Amanda. Last night."

Bobby? Francie takes a minute, tries to process this

name, to identify this person. Bobby. The twin. *Her* twin. But it was Jerry to whom Amanda was engaged!

"What do you mean? I don't understand." She sets down her suitcase, sits on the couch.

"Bobby couldn't handle it, Francie," Liz says. "Graduation coming. His twin brother leaving him. Taking Amanda for his bride. You leaving, flying off in your gorgeous red chariot with Joshua for a weekend of ecstasy. Bill and I planning to move away after graduation when Bill gets out of basic training. I think Bobby just lost his mind completely."

"What did he do?"

"He left a note, that's what. Here—look at it!"

Liz tosses Francie a torn piece of notebook paper. In lead pencil is scribbled the words: "Amanda and I will be married by the time you read this. She will tell you herself that she always wanted me and not Jerry. I'm sorry as hell about all this. Jerry, what can I say? Nothing, only I'm sorry. Bobby."

"Amanda left her engagement ring from Jerry in a teacup on the table," Liz says.

"Did Jerry see the ring there? Did he read Bobby's note?" Only now that the twins are torn from each other, Francie at last finds it possible to call them by their names.

"He saw it, all right. He took it all in and then he . . . just disappeared. Took one of the cars and vanished. Francie, think about these men! Entwined in their mother's womb! She dressed the twins in matching clothes till they were fifteen! They always had the same exact things, the same exact thoughts, the same exact *life*! They never had to exist one day without each other!"

"But they knew they'd have to separate some day, didn't they?"

"I think not. You know, Francie, they were both in love with me. I always felt it."

"Of course, Liz. Everyone knew it. We couldn't *not* know it."

"But when they knew they couldn't have me, they felt there was the still possibility of their having *you*, you or Amanda, the next best choices. Any one of us might do for them, we were all so similar. At the lake, it seemed to be working out so well. All of us were paired. All of us were so happy. Weren't we?"

"I don't think we were so happy, Liz. None of us knew what to think or feel. We were all a little crazed, watching you and Bill practically devouring each other. Of course, we all wanted what you had."

"So, after we came back, you just suddenly drove off for the weekend with Joshua. Don't you think that was a shock to the twins? And then there was only Amanda left, and both twins wanting her. They couldn't divide her, they couldn't both take her."

"Obviously," Francie says.

"But what I don't understand is how Amanda—you know what a good girl Amanda is!—how Amanda could just dump the twin she was engaged to and run off with the other? I know she could hardly tell them apart! But still! What she did makes no sense."

"Life makes no sense, Liz. Did it make sense for you to pretend to be suicidal so you could meet Bill at Peachtree Lake? Did it make sense for me to go off with Joshua . . . and to do what we just did this weekend!"

"Oh, Francie. I didn't even think to *ask* you how it was. I mean, you do look . . . glowing. Are you okay? You don't have to say a word if you don't want to. But I'm dying to ask you—did it hurt? Because it almost killed me the first time. I never told you this, but I had to . . . I had to have some minor surgery first."

"No, it didn't hurt," Francie says. "No pain. Not in any way that I noticed." She can't stifle the smile that now comes, unbidden, to her lips. But she doesn't want to talk about it.

"My God," Liz says. "We're none of us virgins, anymore. No matter how they locked us up, no matter how many rules they laid on our heads, no matter how much they lectured and warned us, we finally escaped at last from the innocence of the Garden of Eden."

"Or at least from the Hazel Wood."

"Oh yes, the Hazel Wood. Because a fire was in my head."

"We were all on fire, Liz."

"I suppose we're not glimmering girls any more, are we?"

"Hardly. Not glimmering girls. More like illuminated women."

"Thank heaven for that," Liz says. "It took a long time coming. But I wonder what made you so brave, suddenly, Francie. . . ."

"I'm not sure," Francie says, picking up her suitcase and beginning to walk down the hall toward her room. "I've just tapped into some new, enormous certainty. I can't explain it any other way. There's just no stopping me now."

# 32

# Land of Hope and Glory

As far as Francie can see, there are black figures wearing gowns and mortarboards. She stands with her fellow graduates at a gateway to the football stadium, in the arch of a high entrance, waiting for the signal to march. The stadium seats reflect a riot of bright colors—women wearing flowered dresses and straw hats, men carrying cushions for the bleachers, everyone holding big cameras and thermoses, waving programs and pennants.

Somewhere in the crush of proud parents, her own are sitting, waiting to see her march to the somber chords of the orchestra, waiting to see her accept the diploma that will certify her to be a fully raised, fully educated, finished child. They, and all the other parents present, will witness their duties formally concluded amid inspirational speeches, exalted songs sung by the choir, and by virtues of age-old finalizing ceremonies taking place under the bright, open vault of the sky.

In the blur that stretches before and behind her, Francie glances at the classmates she has known over the years—friends, fellow Asian flu sufferers, writers of term papers, beer drinkers, panty-raid demonstrators, virgins and nonvirgins, poetry and Russian literature lovers, calculus haters, music appreciators. They, like Francie, have fought to bring themselves to this crossroads, this parting, this place from which they will all be catapulted into the blinding light of the future.

How strange that for this rebirth they wear black, shroud-like garments and cardboard boxes on their heads, the tassels hanging over their eyes. Is there really a moment in time when each person crosses to the next station, assumes the new position, leaves behind the old?

Francie thinks of the markers she has crossed in the past years, none of them clearly drawn on a playing field, none of them achieved before an audience and to a fanfare of drums and music. Yet, she has passed along from one milestone to another, often slowly, sometimes precipitously, half the time resisting change, other times quite unaware that a barrier has come down behind her . . . permanently.

But, still, she's on her journey—one frail human person in this little boat of her life that has been cast on the high seas. Though she doesn't know when storms will strike, or the direction of the wind or the power of the currents, she's got her eyes and hands at the ready, waiting for the moment the helm might come under her control.

Perhaps Dr. Raskolnikov would say she was having an epiphany! She shifts her weight, glad that she is wearing not high heels but instead her comfortable flats, as she scans the crowd again, trying to find the real people from her life.

There, one section beside hers, she sees Harvey Rubin. He's got a sly grin on his face—Francie thinks it's because he's just learned for sure he's been given a trust fund by his parents that will earn him $5,000 a year . . . he may not ever have to get a job!

A few rows down she sees Amanda's brilliant blonde curls under the mortarboard. Amanda, having married very suddenly indeed (this marriage virus having taken so many of her friends, as well), has come back to graduate in time, with Bobby (somewhere out there, too, tall and lanky in his cap and gown) getting his degree in engineering.

Jerry has disappeared. Francie has known for some days now that he dropped out of school and traveled back to Peachtree Lake, where he arranged to go into the boat and fishing business with his Georgia neighbor, Bailey. Jerry's parents gave him the deed to the cottage;

not half the deed, not half the cottage—but the whole of it.

Rows below, Francie can see the familiar roundness of Mary Ella's shoulders, that sturdy, goodhearted girl about to march into her life of good works and good deeds. Her conviction that for every pot there is a cover has been borne out. Mary Ella is in love, and for her happy endings abound. Perhaps it's just the heat of the sun or the emotion of the moment, but Francie feels as if a happy ending is engulfing her, too, as it might at the end of a powerful film when the music swells and "The End" appears upon the screen.

As if to affirm this, a loud, powerful drum roll sounds. Those holding graduation programs as fans flutter wildly them wildly, like the beating wings of birds. Then silence falls over the stadium as the first notes of Elgar's "Pomp and Circumstance" rise upward from the orchestra on the playing field.

At the same instant, someone sets loose a cluster of pastel balloons. Francie watches them rise and dot the sky like so many souls set free until she feels the procession begin to move, very slowly. All the rows of graduates begin to march forward from every archway in the stadium, down every ramp, step by measured step, down toward the field, where rows of black metal chairs wait to receive them.

Beneath her, Francie thinks she can see Liz, or at least the graceful, singular slant of her head, her shining hair barely visible under the square hat. Bill, the soldier, has gotten leave for this event, coming as it does at the end of basic training, and tonight the two of them will leave together for California, where he will be stationed.

Francie, having no husband, no job, no deed to any house, plans to go home very briefly with her parents. The blessed news came two days ago from New York: she will be leaving soon to work at *Mademoiselle*!

She scans the crowd, looking for Joshua, who is up front somewhere in the group of graduates favored with "High Honors with Special Distinction." This is one step above her own "High Honors"—but Francie is quite satisfied with her achievement. Later tonight, she will meet Joshua's parents, and he will meet hers. She and Joshua have agreed to introduce their parents informally. Only the two of them know how inextricably their lives are wound, beyond measure. They have fortified themselves for the long haul and are in agreement about what it will take to achieve their reunion. Who knows? Joshua may one day play with an orchestra far greater than this earnest one on the field, bringing all its powers to the refrain that reverberates now through the air: "Land of hope and glory . . ."

Her fellow graduates are coming down to the field from all directions, spilling out like an ebony river across the grass, their heads held high, mortarboards straight, tassels swinging. Their gowns shimmer in the sunlight like the iridescent feathers of black starlings.

Francie looks to the side and recognizes her parents not five feet from her. They don't know she is just abreast of them as they strain to find her in the thousands of figures below. But suddenly they turn toward each other. She sees it happen, the primal thing. Her parents kiss, deeply and sweetly in the radiance of some joy that perhaps is due in part to her existence.

She passes them by, moves beyond them.

*"Wider still and wider, shall our bounds be set . . .*
*God who made us mighty, make us mightier yet . . ."*

Francie is not so sure about God's having had anything to do with it, but something is definitely going on here, something shattering and monumental enough to bring tears to her eyes. She can't say she isn't mightily impressed.

**Library of American Fiction**
The University of Wisconsin Press Fiction Series

Marleen S. Barr
*Oy Pioneer! A Novel*

Dodie Bellamy
*The Letters of Mina Harker*

Melvin Jules Bukiet
*Stories of an Imaginary Childhood*

Andrew Furman
*Alligators May Be Present*

Merrill Joan Gerber
*Glimmering Girls: A Novel of the Fifties*

Rebecca Goldstein
*The Dark Sister*

Rebecca Goldstein
*Mazel*

Jesse Lee Kercheval
*The Museum of Happiness*

Alan Lelchuk
*American Mischief*

Alan Lelchuk
*Brooklyn Boy*

Curt Leviant
*Ladies and Gentlemen, The Original Music of the Hebrew Alphabet*
   and *Weekend in Mustara*

David Milofsky
*A Friend of Kissinger: A Novel*

Lesléa Newman
*A Letter to Harvey Milk: Short Stories*

Mordecai Roshwald
*Level 7*

Lewis Weinstein
*The Heretic: A Novel*